One Day
in April

for Yvonne
with my
best Wishes
j 2011

One Day in April

JAD EL HAGE

QUARTET BOOKS

First published in 2011 by
Quartet Books Limited
A member of the Namara Group
27 Goodge Street, London WIT 2LD

A catalogue record for this book
is available from the British Library

ISBN   978 0 7043 7237 5

Typeset by Antony Gray
Printed and bound in Great Britain by
T J International Ltd, Padstow, Cornwall

No painting or drawing, however naturalist, belongs to its subject in the way a photograph does.

JOHN BERGER

The afternoon knows what the morning never suspected.

Swedish proverb

Prologue

You could say I was destined to become a photographer. Uncle Varouj believes that being an Armenian photographer in Lebanon is the most natural thing in the world, as natural as the cedar tree on the flag. 'Armenians are photography, just as the cedar tree is Lebanon!' he says. He taught me to trust my instincts and look at the world as a series of clicks. 'Aim and shoot, Koko, let your eyes do the work.'

I was born in the Armenian suburb of Bourj Hammoud, north of Beirut, in 1948. I dropped out of school at the age of twelve. Schools at that time were poorly funded, badly equipped, housed in tin-roofed shacks and designed to incarcerate the maximum number of street urchins. Those who managed to obtain a genuine education were the ones with devoted parents waiting for them at home to mend the damage done by the school. Unfortunately, mine had died before I started kindergarten. After school the kids were picked up by their parents, all except Koko. Brothers and sisters held hands and went home singing or quarrelling. I walked home alone, except for the times when a tomboy called Arsiné, who lived down the road from us, would suddenly grip my hand as if she were capturing it for keeps.

The insult that followed the injury of my parents' death took the form of a teacher armed with a wooden ruler. His intoxication with the clap of that ruler against our soft skin dwarfed his meagre teaching skills. I endured him until I mustered enough resolve to drop out altogether, and went to help my uncle in his Photoshop.

I learned my trade through trial and error. The minute my

lens is focused, a new chemistry begins to stir. I'm not sure how or why, but I get signals, like Morse code. Faces, places, incidents, accidents, ugliness and beauty – all are engaged in a dialogue with time, light, and the perfect frame. Unlike the naked eye, what the lens captures is stilled forever. The naked eye is subject to emotions, to partiality, to its own selectiveness, which is prone to distortion and possibly to oblivion. But a well-clicked photo is a witness to one particular, unique moment.

I once read that a famous English poet believed photography brought a new sadness to the world. Perhaps because photos have their limitations. There's an element of finality sealing them; their immunity to change is a cold answer to the eye's hunger for more meat, more life. Or perhaps he didn't look that good in photos. But I've noticed that browsing through old sepias and black and whites from my uncle's albums gives me a sensation akin to apparition: Armenians in their coarse attire, their thick moustaches, their deep eyes, sitting with their head-scarved women and jumbled-up children, staring at the lens – here we are, take us to immortality! If I look at them long enough the carpet of time is drawn from under my feet. A whole factory of memories and quasi memories goes into motion. Time ferments the deposit of life in all of them. They stop me in my tracks, draw me back years and continents to look and see again.

In those albums is the history of a people who go back thousands of years. Like Lebanon and Palestine, Armenia was repeatedly occupied by large empires: Persian, Arab, Ottoman, not to mention recurring attacks by hordes of Turkic and Mongolian tribesmen. As a regional hot spot it was disputed, raided, and invaded by ruthless armies. Diaspora became a normal extension of Armenian history. After the First World War thousands of Armenians were uprooted, mainly from Anatolia. Over one million were killed. The dislocated sought refuge in Syria, Lebanon, Egypt, Iraq and other Levantine countries.

My uncle's albums include pictures taken during the exodus, of families harbouring in barns and stables or sleeping in the bush or on river banks. The determined and sometimes defiant stare in the eyes of their children is identical to those I've seen in the Palestinian refugee camps. There are also pictures of weddings and christenings and school groups, among them a few clicks from my early childhood.

But the one I love most is a snapshot of my parents that hung on the living room wall above my sofa-bed. It was taken in Beirut's centre, a quick click by an Armenian street photographer of a couple walking together arm in arm. The lady's coat is partly open and the gentleman's free hand is comfortably tucked in his pocket. My dad had been a jeweller and watchmaker. He inherited his trade from his forefathers, who were famous in Cilicia for their precision and honesty. My mum was French educated. She came from a prominent Cilician family. Her sophisticated hairdo and European clothes set her apart from the rugged Armenian refugees I see in Uncle's albums. I often wondered how she coped, as a child, with the long journey on foot by the Euphrates. I spent hours diving into their faces, trying to imagine my life with them, how it would have been in a different home, with brothers and sisters and birthdays and parties. Trying to remember what I was like when I had them and what they were like when they had me.

My recurring dreams of my parents derive from images of other children with their parents. Seeing myself hugged and kissed and given presents and pushed in a pram on a nice sunny day are not necessarily my own memories. They are clicks by my inner lens of a life that never was and never will be. Whenever I asked Aunty Clauda about my parents, her eyes would just go misty and she would brush my face gently with her rough fingers. 'It was an accident, Koko. A speeding car lost its brakes while they were crossing the Corniche.' My uncle would only say, 'They were regular God-fearing Armenians, son, bless their souls.' Putting a firm lid on painful memories is a trait of the Armenian Diaspora. The idea is to instil pride rather than bitterness. At first it was a coping mechanism against their traumatic genocide. Then it became part of their culture.

In 1965 Uncle Varouj had a minor stroke. He was getting on a bit anyway and decided this was a good time for me to take over his shop. But I was too young. I needed to be out. While he was recovering, I spent my time wandering, clicking my days away. One afternoon I went up on a roof and clicked an aeroplane carrying the sunset on its back over Beirut's concrete jungle. It was good. I printed it, put it on the top of my best shots and took it to the *Daily Sun*. Fathy Nawar, the feature editor, gave it this prophetic caption: Memories of days to come: the sun sets on freedom? It caught the eye of the boss and landed me my job. I was seventeen. Receiving my first pay cheque, with the boss shaking my hand, was an unforgettable moment: 'You are a real Armenian, Krikor; your pictures are good to look at and they tell a story. That's what we need. Welcome to the *Daily Sun*.'

The boss assigned me to Emile Khoury, his 'Field Marshal', as he called him. Considering the bickering and bitching that plagues the click people, I was lucky that Emile took a shine to me. 'Capa, Koko!' he exclaimed when he first saw me. I had no idea then who Capa was, he whose best shots covered the wall above Emile's desk along with a portrait of the legend himself in a Humphrey Bogart pose, cigarette at one corner of his lips. Emile was right – I do bear some resemblance to the American war photographer lionised by Hollywood: the same bridged eyebrows, the same thick black hair (though mine is wavier) and the same thin lips.

'See this one?' Emile laid a fraternal hand on my shoulder and pointed at a picture of a Spanish Civil War rebel taken at the very moment he was shot: falling back, his rifle about to drop from his hand, all alone in the middle of an empty space. 'That's not the click of a passer-by or a tourist but an insider from the belly of the beast. I could die for a shot like that,' Emile sighed. A coloured portrait of Casablanca's heroine was pasted up near Capa's. 'Look at her, Koko, just oozing sensuality. Ingrid fell in love with him in Paris after the war.' He slapped my shoulder: 'Make it in the killing fields and the dames will die for you!' he rasped, in a poor imitation of Bogie's gravelly voice.

It was my first day of work, and the first day of my new life.

Beirut

13 April 1977

Morning

1

Nishan walked his first solo steps this morning. No crawling, no bum-gliding, he made the shift from hand-help to free waddle. Flipping his arms, he pushed his neck forward and toddled across the living room, a penguin heading for his first dip. This little miracle made Arsiné forget her morning habits and lose herself in merriment. I lost myself too, playing with Nishan for half an hour when I should have been driving to work. Even as I drove to work, I shut out the world around me, musing that one ought to have the day off when ones child becomes Homo erectus. The image of Nishan's wobbling nappies and chubby little legs even spared me the usual disgust when negotiating my way through the wreckage of war torn Beirut.

When I reached the *Daily Sun* offices a couple of minutes before nine, an eerie hush permeated the editorial section commonly known as the manger. Calm was uncharacteristic for this time of day when the scribes were usually shuffling telex sheets, cutting and distributing material, discussing priorities and recounting brushes with death. Generally this was a fizzy time of day. Instead, most people were avoiding eye contact. Some mumbled Good-Morning under their breath. A few female reporters were huddled in a corner sniffling. I'm sure I heard one of them sob. It could be anything, I thought. People are falling like flies everywhere, day and night. If someone is hurt, the general consensus is to wait until you are told. If one of us is killed then it's a different scene altogether. Someone will be at the entrance to let you know. The media had already lost twenty three members since the beginning of the civil war, three of them from the *Daily Sun*.

I was late, so I didn't expect to find Emile or anyone else in the photo department. And frankly, I didn't want to hear bad news, not yet anyway.

My roster read: 'Out of town assignment.' Fathy Nawar, the feature editor, had written on a post-it note: 'Go to Dyarna, nine km north of Baalbek. There's no signpost. Look for seven cypress trees on the right. Take the dirt track upwards. The village is home to a dozen fugitives including some ex-cons who released themselves when the prisons were abandoned. They're organising a huge wedding. Catch up with Nader Abi Nader – he's writing the story. Give me a scoop like you did with Raml.'

I'd been the only photojournalist to get into the Raml prison when the convicts were preparing to flee. It had indeed been a scoop. Never before had anyone managed to take a shot inside that Ottoman-style gaol, let alone photograph its inmates. *Exodus into Unsafe Freedom but Freedom Nevertheless* had been Fathy's headline, spread across eight columns crowning my shots of men releasing themselves into the hell of the civil war. What had happened to them? Ex-cons celebrating a sumptuous wedding in the context of this ruinous war would be a great angle. And for any of us, an out of town assignment these days was a welcome bonus. We'd been smelling human and animal combustion, dodging snipers, rushing to car bomb sites, following kidnappings, clicking foreign envoys and Arab delegations galore for the last two years, so a story like this would certainly be a breather. What I didn't understand was choosing Nader to write the words. Nader, of all people. Fathy couldn't have forgotten how much I hated this guy. It's a small town in a small country; everyone's connected, especially those in the same trade. Fathy knew all about my clashes with Nader. He knew about Najla, and the Blue Pirate and the book of photos. Did he think that forcing us together would produce a piece 'with a sharp edge,' as he liked to say?

But sharp edges are everywhere. For example, a few days ago: I jump into a military jeep heading to the airport to click the special envoy of The Arab League – he's been canvassing between Cyprus and Beirut for nearly three months and after every visit repeating the same refrain about national unity, end of hostilities and the bloody Cairo pact. But sudden shelling aborts my mission. Safety measures taken on the spot by the military deviate my journey towards a barrack in the southern town of Hadath. Now I hear on the radio that my target is being diverted to Chtaura. I need a shot of His Excellency stepping out from the chopper. But how to get to Chtaura? While I'm thinking, the soldiers insist I have lunch with them, so I eat lentil soup and a slice of kebbeh with the guardians of the flag. Enter an awesome commandant. They stir. 'As you were. Bon appétit,' he says. Then he takes me under his powerful wing. In no time we are riding in a chopper to Chtaura. This country is so beautiful from the sky. 'It must have fallen from heaven by mistake,' he says. What a waste, what a shame it's been destroyed by its own people, etcetera, etcetera. Hey, here comes another bird. The commandant radios his colleague. Unbelievable! – the envoy is on board! Come closer! I become click-crazed. The two helicopters manoeuvre to bring me as close as they can. Click, click, gotcha! And the caption reads: Arab Initiative in the Air! Sharp edge accomplished.

I grabbed my tools and left the photo department. I pressed the lift's button from the fourth to the ground floor but first it went up to the sixth to let the boss in. Ustaz Burhan entered and pressed G, totally ignoring my presence. Not even a Good Morning. This was really weird, it had never happened before. Usually he beams when he sees me. He calls me Krikor, my son.

I'm practically a part of his family. So what on earth is going on today?

A couple of seconds later the electricity went off and we were stranded. Nothing unusual there. Being stranded in a dead elevator is so common these days that it makes an uninterrupted ride a happy event. But still the boss didn't move, didn't even seem to see me. His face was shut down, his eyes vacant to the world. He was standing so close I could count his slow breaths, yet there were continents between us.

I longed to tell him about Nishan's first steps, wanted him to relate the news to his daughter Manal during his daily phone call to Paris. But whatever was bugging him, I could feel it snuffing out my own words. I could only stare at the floor, at his perfectly pressed grey trousers and his shiny black shoes. Sure I'd seen him disgruntled before, sarcastic, even furious. But right or wrong, he was Burhan Sadik, the man who had opened the door to my career.

I craned my neck to read the headline of today's issue gripped under his arm: Two Years Since The Bus Massacre. I felt a pinch of guilt for not remembering the gruesome anniversary, especially as it's so close to the Armenian genocide memorial ten days later. My head had been so brimming with the joy of seeing Nishan walk that it had slipped my mind to listen to the news. And Arsiné, instead of turning on the radio as usual, had collapsed with laughter and then run to phone her mother. But how could this memory lapse make me a stranger to my boss?

I tried to understand. Chaos has its own mind-boggling, ever-changing agenda. Two days ago the boss shook the country with his weekly editorial. He was not hopeful. He wrote like the blind Homer describing hell and damnation: 'This is the most dishonourable war, the ugliest, the dirtiest. A rat's nest of wars and revolutions all in one. An Israeli war while Lebanon slept on the soft pillow of guaranteed treaties and international protection. An Arab-Arab war: the war of all Arabs who never had the chance to fight against each other so they chose the Lebanese arena instead. The war of Palestinian against Palestinian, against the whole world, and against Lebanon where their hopes and aspirations had flourished for the first time since the Nakba. And the war of the Lebanese: their frustrated revolts, their cumulative dissatisfactions, their sectarian grudges. And this war will continue. Even when some people think it's over it will continue, because every gang has its heroes and martyrs and the insatiable need to invent ever more heroes and more martyrs.'

He got it off his chest and then came to the editorial meeting cheerful and merry, regaling us with tales of Manal and her Parisian adventures.

Try to understand.

A terrible thought hit me: had the boss finally found out about my cut of the ransom from his kidnapping? A sickening chill of shame and panic rose in me at the memory.

It happened about a year ago. I'd worked late one night and decided to stay over at the next-door hotel. Emile and other members of the staff had been living there ever since the roads to their homes were cut off. It was one of many strategies that kept the *Daily Sun* rising despite the civil war. So I phoned Arsiné, made sure she was OK, then took a hot shower and tried to get some sleep through the thudding of mortars.

Not long before dawn, when slumber was finally embalming my stiff limbs, I was propelled out of bed by a bang at the door, the type usually used by the Secret Service.

'Who's there?' I called out hoarsely.

'Emile. Open up!'

I sleep naked year round, can't bear a thread, not even the underwear I couldn't find in my haste to answer the door. 'What's wrong?'

'Cover your soujouk and follow me downstairs.'

Emile was barefoot in boxer shorts and sling tee-shirt, his hair peaked atop his head from sleep. He was obviously shaken.

In the lobby half the newspaper staff was gathered, fidgeting as if about to be deported. Not all of them were regular residents, which explained Emile's agitation; for staff to drive here from both sides of the divided city at this hour meant mega mess. Blood hit my temples like a hammer.

'Krikor!' they cried in unison, surging towards me.

'What the fuck – '

'The boss – he's been kidnapped! The kidnappers called. They want you to go get him. They specified you by name. And they sent this note.'

Not that this was delivered in anything resembling speech; more like a herd of troubled animals unburdening their fear, concern, and envy – why Krikor? Someone handed me the note, scribbled in Armenian on a napkin. Another plunged an envelope inside my jacket. Still numbed with sleep, I looked at the napkin, read it, read it again, striving to keep my face blank despite my fear and puzzlement. The civil war had been spitting out all kinds of lunatics, ranging from a messiah who crosses the warring zones barefoot collecting orphans, to cannibals huddled in the rubble barbecuing their enemies. And certainly anyone able to buy or steal a gun can use it to make money. But these guys had kidnapped a soft target and asked for an affordable ransom. Clever: no need to make it public and risk the life of a remarkable man, just be realistic and pay up. Given the senselessness of everything else, this scheme was looking more and more like a joy ride in your big sister's car.

My silence infuriated the group but I'd already decided not to divulge the most bizarre part of the message. All I said was, 'I'll go. Emile drives. He stays in the car a couple of blocks away. I walk. I know the area like the back of my hand.'

I didn't wait for approval. Nor did Emile. He flew to his room and came back dressed in a minute.

As soon as we set off, I took out the envelope and counted the money: seventy-thousand liras. Cheap, but smart.

Emile was beginning to lose his cool. 'Where are we going?'

'My place first. I have to fetch something,' I lied.

'What? I have a gun on –'

'No. Leave it in the car. And be patient, we may be getting a cut from this.' I was beginning to feel good about myself, as good as when planning my little robberies in Bourj Hammoud.

Emile was about to start thumping me for my uncharacteristic calm, so I had to tell him. When he heard what was on the napkin, he almost killed us. 'I want to see this,' he crowed, hitting the steering wheel with both hands. He lost control of the car and galloped it over a broken pavement.

'No, we'll play it by the book,' I said. 'And be vigilant, just in case it's a trap.'

When we arrived in Sayfeh, Emile parked the car in a strategic corner overlooking our living room balcony. He was to interfere only if I put the balcony light on once; twice meant everything is OK. He loaded his Beretta and punched my shoulder good luck.

I walked to my own home feeling like a thief about to break into a stranger's house. With every step I was fending off more and more dark thoughts. I kept touching the money in my jacket and wanting it to stop being there. My doubts rose to a disturbing level. I slowed down. Those hundred metres to my house were becoming the longest walk of my life, but I couldn't chicken out now. I wished I had taken the pistol from Emile, if only for the feel of it close to my hand. I stopped a short distance from our apartment building and scanned the parked cars on both sides of the street. I knew all of them except one black Range Rover with a flickering blue sensor and more antennae than a radio station. My kneecaps softened. They're here. Should I go back and get that pistol? But the image that finally thrust me forward at speed was Arsiné all alone with a bunch of weirdoes.

I opened the door as casually as possible. The coffee aroma

beckoned me. I took a long sniff and felt better. Arsiné doesn't smoke, doesn't drink to excess, but she needs her lifeline of coffee. 'Cut my caffeine, I'd walk to Brazil for a cup,' she once said.

She was in her dressing gown, sleepily relaxed, her short bob neatly combed, sitting there drinking coffee with three hooded men. Her 'guests' wore black from top to toe. Even their little machine guns were black. They stood up. She came over to hug me. I hugged her back, hardly breathing. Then I shook hands with the hoods. Arsiné poured me a coffee. I picked it up and sipped, still standing. I strived to keep my cool. They were in my house. They had the guns, I had their money. No one can tell what might trigger violence nowadays. So, easy went Koko. One of the men spoke Armenian to me. He apologised for the inconvenience. I said nothing. He moved into small talk: his father (he wouldn't say his name) knew my Uncle Varouj. And he just loved my shots. Arsiné poured more coffee, smiling encouragingly at me. Now the others began talking. How did I become a photojournalist? What's it like being out there on the edge of death every day? Did I bring the money? They were so laid-back the situation surpassed mere surrealism. We could easily have been old friends in a dream where mates visit wearing black balaclavas and sporting automatic rifles.

Then Arsiné said nonchalantly, 'Give me the money, Koko. And go to the bedroom.'

'What's in the bedroom?'

'Your boss,' the Armenian said. 'He's tied up.'

'Who are you people?'

'Friends,' another answered, yawning.

Arsiné whispered, 'They're not political. They pretend. They give a lot away to the needy, and they play it safe.'

'I don't get it. Put it in plain Armenian.'

'We are independent.' The tallest of the three spoke at last, stretching his legs under my coffee table, like my brother if I had one. 'We operate on the fringe of the big festival, you might say.'

I took heart. 'But we're now accomplices to a serious kidnapping here,' I said. 'What's in it for us?'

'Ten percent,' the man said.

'Ten thousand. I have expenses.'

'Done.'

I gave the envelope to Arsiné. 'I want you all out of here in five. What do you call yourselves, by the way?'

'Black Snow.'

The minute I opened the door to our bedroom, I despised myself and loathed those ten thousand liras. I vowed to pay it back somehow. For, by the light of a candle on the dressing table, I saw my boss. They had tied Ustaz Burhan to the radiator and taped his mouth shut. His eyes cried for me. He was in his white night jellabia – they must have taken him straight from his bed. I walked over to him and freed first his mouth and then his hands.

'Krikor! My son!'

I took him in my arms.

Until then I'd been feeling rather amused – the note had read: We are waiting for you where the best coffee is served. Come alone. But the joke ceased to be funny when my boss started sobbing. He broke my heart so suddenly I could only reply with tears. I mean, he wasn't just any old boss. This was the man who had plucked me from the slums and given me a career.

I comforted him as best I could and brought him to the living room. The hooded men were standing by the door about to leave. They had the nerve to bow and apologise. Arsiné slammed the door behind them.

Suddenly the familiar jolt. The elevator trembled and landed us in the foyer, still like strangers who never met before.

2

In my car I fingerprinted a kiss on Nishan's little picture on the dashboard – wish your father a good day, son – and drove off, taking side streets, trying my best to get out of Beirut as quickly as possible; escaping the shaming shadow of Burhan Sadik. Most checkpoints knew my VW and waved me through straightaway; power of the fourth estate, you might say. But I got snagged in a demo at the Tayouneh roundabout, close to where the bus massacre had happened two years ago. I saw Emile doing his Nikon fox trot: now you see him, now you don't. I couldn't get out of the car. The honking was maddening and the air was blue with squabbles between those demonstrators who favoured opening a passage for the traffic and others who insisted on blocking the road. They were pathetically disorganised. I sensed exhaustion and despair beneath the aggression. There was no one to aim this demo at. Not even the local militias deigned to come out, only people who had lost loved ones on that infamous day. Plus perhaps a few from the dying species of Conscientious Objector, holding banners demanding another dying value, Justice, and displaying blown-up photos of the victims. Some of the photos were Emile's.

Theoretically, I had covered the bus massacre with Emile. But the truth is, I'd been shocked into immobility when we arrived at the scene. Normally I ignore my feet. Having to click away while moving forward, backward, up stairs and through alley-ways, into crowds and between cars, I move as if invisibly winged. Suddenly my feet had become dead weights. While Emile circulated like a high voltage wire between the bodies and the police and the onlookers and the crazed women, I was rooted to the spot. A chunk of me was lying on the ground, riddled with bullets, open-mouthed, eyes staring at the vast emptiness of death with those twenty-six Palestinian refugees. The rest of me was naked among hostile, deeply troubled strangers. They shoved and gestured at a bus stained with blood and shreds of clothes, at the victims of their narrow beliefs and blind hatred. I became aware of a strange odour. Unidentifiable, yet strongly present. I had no clue then that freshly-slain humans smelled. A powerful yet oddly abstract smell. Like that of rocks or clouds. Was it the quickly-drying blood on the asphalt? Or the hollow air gurgling through their silent throats? Or the smell of their aborted day, their severed dreams. A sense of alienation lifted me up out of Ein al-Rumaneh and deposited me inside the long-ago Armenian massacre. Those same *turks* were hauling dirt over my dead body. I shivered. A layer was peeling off my skin. I didn't belong in this country any more. Mentally, I shredded my Lebanese ID.

Back home that night, Arsiné had tried to alleviate my devastation. 'You're being irrational, Koko, denouncing the whole country because of a handful of psychopaths.'

'So what? I'm comfortable being just plain Armenian, like all those other foreign photojournalists drinking vodka martinis at the Commodore Hotel and musing about the Lebos and their horrific antics and then going to sleep dreaming of their own countries, their sane countries.'

'There you go! Plumbing your genetic subconscious. Remembering Armenia when you've never even been to Armenia. Look at all the other Lebanese we know who carry two and sometimes three IDs, just to fool the different groups. Emile, for example – he has documents from every organisation under the sun. It doesn't bother him. He doesn't lose a "peel" of skin. He wakes up every morning as Emile Khoury, Maronite from Amchit. Whatever other names and religions he has to embody during the day are irrelevant to him, no more important than the dirty socks he sheds at night. He speaks the dialects of the land, and he takes the piss out of each of them, including his own. He's fine. Phone him, see if he wants to change his name after what happened. Identity isn't something we discard like a broken chair. We were born here, Koko. We went to school here. We voted for the first time here. And we were given an ID with the cedar tree here. Armenia is nothing but a dreamland, Koko. We are Lebanese.'

'Armenian, Arsiné!' I cried.

Why can't I change? People change their religion. They change their looks, their politics. I wasn't changing much, just denying the imposition of circumstances. Fuck the Pasha, as my uncle is always saying; if he hadn't sent his army to kill my grandparents I would have inherited a beautiful house and a thriving jewellery shop. My fingers, they're dyed not with gold and silver powders but with stinking developer. It doesn't matter what's floating in the tray in the darkness of my dark room – pretty women on the beach with demolition-ball boobs or hooded militias, they all swim like garbage in the tray. Then I rescue them. I baptise them in the fixer. I lift them to the light and I dry them. Back in the glare of daylight, Koko the Armenian photojournalist is damn good. Why does everyone else stress the issue of ethnicity if I'm just Lebanese? Why the Armenian this and the Armenian that, when we're all basking under the same cedar tree? And why mock us when some of us speak Armenian-Arabic, mixing up the genders, turning Arabic into a unisex joke? Ask any dickhead about Armenian culture, what do they know? A few words they picked up from Bourj Hammoud and scraps about our political parties and our football teams, and everyone gets them muddled. Do they know what happened to us? Why we are here? Why we are scattered all over the globe? Have they any idea of our contribution to the making of this country? Shoemakers, dressmakers, carpenters, electricians, artists, printers, you name it, but above all the photographers who roamed this land with their tripod cameras capturing the happy moments of life. I grew up aspiring to become like Manoug, who took the best shots ever of Baalbek and the white peaks of Sannine. No one before him had ever managed to crystallise the beauty of this country with such magic clicks. Now he's been kicked out, all the way to Canada. Did anyone scream: No, not Manoug? Fuck the Pasha, I keep saying to myself as I go and click roll upon roll of film, as if history is tattooed on my genes. As if Jamal Pasha is just down the road, smoking his water pipe and planning massacres. This is not my land. It doesn't remember me. Its collective memory is selective. Every gang has its own history, its own interpretation of events, its own stake, so what you see is never what you get. You see people looking alike as they eat the same hummus, but scratch the surface and what do you get? Enemies. The proof is April 13, 1975. Stop! Out! Shoot! Kill them all! Why? Because they're Palestinians. They could have been Armenians, Kurds, Syrians, Assyrians, Syriacs, you name it. Everybody is here. A melting pot of fugitives from everywhere, yet they all claim exclusive rights and special privileges. If those who committed that massacre believe they are Lebanese plus, then I am Lebanese minus.

Arsiné and I had carried on talking about this identity business long into the night, our river of words rolling on and on against the darkness, unconcerned by the dawn looming up from the pit of uncertainties. Our balcony sniffed a meandering breeze from the port of Beirut, no different from other balconies across the narrow road, all webbed with electricity and telephone wires, washing lines, wilting plants and the rusting toys of the fast-aging children of ancient Lebanon.

How could all this have ended up in today's pathetic little demonstration? Do we forget because we can't bear to remember, because the truth would crush us? Or is it all a part of survival because reality surpasses our worst nightmares?

Soon the demonstration was disintegrating like a sand castle washed by waves. A few disgruntled youths kicked cars, smashed road signs and spat in frustration before wandering away, leaving nothing behind but a meek echo of one day in April, two years ago. Except then the wound was fresher and the emotions higher and the dead were still alive.

3

I was trying to find Beirut's Armenian news station on my car radio when Emile's head popped through my window: 'Heading east, are we?'

'Shit, man, you scared me!'

'Lucky bugger.'

'Swap? Nishan walked today, I'd rather stay here with him.'

'Did you see the boss?'

'Yeah, in the elevator. He seemed in a terrible mood.'

'Didn't you hear the news?' Emile's face darkened. His eyes darted away from me for a second. 'Manal was killed in a car accident in Paris last night.'

'No!'

'Go to the Bekaa. Trust me; Fathy is doing you a favour.' Emile slung his bag over his shoulder and trotted off.

I sank into my car seat.

Manal's life sprang out before me in a stream of tears. I'd clicked her school performances, her birthdays and her parties. I'd liked her from the first time I saw her: a little olive-skinned ballerina, maybe eight or nine, in her white tutu, dancing around her absent father's desk while a tape recorder issued orders in French. She doesn't see me open the door. Automatically I click her. A second click frames her startled face. A third, her grin. She feigns a bird in flight. I move like a twister clicking her non-stop. The shot that captured her flying from the leather sofa, charging at my lens, ended up in pride of place on her father's desk.

She was utterly physical, difficult to keep still. Even when stilled, she was a cheetah poised to leap. I believed she was going to become a great ballerina – dancing suited her desire to dazzle. 'Good' upset her. 'Fantastic' was OK. But words were not sufficient: the best way to react to her performance was to clap, wave, jump up and down. Her passion was compelling. It swept me up in its wake.

A few years after that first encounter, I found her in the basement print room, raising her thin voice above the din of machinery in a heated debate with the chief mechanic. She was wearing blue dungarees and a small triangular scarf and waving her arms about, saying she wanted to use the print room after hours to stage a dance project. The chief was objecting: the floor is uneven, it's dangerous, the insurance won't cover it, there's no free time for rehearsals, etcetera.

'You finish printing at four in the morning,' she argued. 'I'll bring my music then and rehearse. And then just give me twenty minutes on Sunday to present the show. My teacher and two other judges will come to see me, that's all, I promise.'

The chief was having none of it.

Then she saw me and jumped at me for back-up.

I took her to one side. 'Does your father know about this?'

'Yes, he said to persuade the chief, it's his ship. Now are you going to help me or what?'

'Why do you want to do it in this dungeon, for God's sake?'

'Industrial versus natural. I'll be doing bits of *Swan Lake*, you see what I mean?'

'I know a better place. Trust me.'

I took her to the oldest print house in Beirut, a place that had recently been transformed into a museum with modern lighting, a small stage and a screen for projection. She loved it and gave me a swirling hug that almost had us both crashing down.

Unfortunately, it all got out of hand. Word spread. Uninvited media came, turned a school project into a debut. Manal rose from schoolgirl to celebrity overnight. Suddenly she was in demand. She danced at the prestigious Baalbek festival. She featured in avant-garde plays and co-starred in a musical.

'You propelled those tender wings into stormy weather, Krikor,' the boss told me, part proud, part apprehensive.

Then she was chosen, along with three other prodigies, to attend a workshop at the school of Maurice Béjart in Paris.

'Maurice Béjart, Papa, Maurice Béjart!' Manal was aflame.

'Are you sure you're ready for such a tough regime? Ballet at that level needs discipline and obedience.'

'It needs passion, Papa, passion!'

'She'll be all right. Let her go, boss.'

Now the enthusiasm I'd had for Manal's talent was crushing my chest. Like a sphinx her father had been standing beside me in the elevator for what, three, five minutes? Could I have stood like that? Could I imagine Nishan killed and just put on my suit and go to work tucking my newspaper under my arm? No wonder he couldn't utter a word. What could he possibly say? 'Good morning Krikor, Manal died last night, how are you?' Or maybe remind me of propelling her tender wings into a storm? Did I? Was I truly a part of Manal's final destiny? With my modest help or without it, wasn't she going her own way? Wasn't she simply a force of nature? All I did was take her by the hand from one printing house to another. Her success, her ascent to stardom and her Paris dream coming true, these were all her achievements. She was the show, I only clicked the pictures. But you let a child go to the beach for a nice swim and she drowns. Take her to the zoo and she's mauled by a gorilla. Somewhere inside, justified or not, you feel the unbearable weight of guilt.

I sat in my stationary car, all thoughts of my assignment gone, listening to radio interviews with arts commentators expressing their feelings over Manal's loss: gripping performances, great talent, terrible fate. 'Which loss is more tragic: youth or the dreams of youth? If the wind breaks a branch laden with fruit

before it is ripe, do we mourn the branch or the wasted crop?'
Her dance teacher was trying hard to say something deep before
breaking down in muffled sobs.

Futile questions about reversing what cannot be reversed are
alien to me. It would have paralysed my whole life, trying to
turn the clock back every time something went wrong. Sure,
there are moments when a failure pricks my memory and makes
me shudder, but I chase it out. I move away from it, scolding
my weakness. Now, though, I was feeling helpless and guilty. I
was loathing the times I'd spent developing Manal's pictures,
contemplating them, comparing them with previous ones, discussing them with Emile before deciding which to show the
boss. I was dreading coming back to the few pasted up next to
my war shots, placed there to ease the edge of our daily violence.

I could hear forlorn Armenian hymns. At first they sounded
like ripples from afar, echoes lurking in a dream. I adjusted the
radio and closed my eyes as the crescendo rose ever higher.
Manal's white tutu floated into my imagination. She enters our
church, pirouetting down the aisle all the way to the altar. The
dark miniatures of saints and apostles glow. The pale flicker of
candles shiver in the clouds of incense. The crowd chants
fervently, Sourp! Sourp! Holy! Holy! And Manal keeps twirling
until she disappears through the dome of angels.

4

April is the cruellest month indeed, the month of genocide, when Armenians throughout the world remember their massacred forefathers, and now the Palestinians have added it to their half-century list of tragedies. Not to mention the Bahr El Baqar massacre of thirty Egyptian school children by Israeli napalm bombers, the eighth of April six years ago. Yet despite all this, it's still the time of year when the earth exhales a kaleidoscope of flowers, making amends for the greyness of winter. I drew a breath of relief from the few unscathed blooms between the derelict buildings along the road. Out of Beirut, there were fewer road blocks, fewer militias, fewer walls sprayed with bullets. My eyes took a break from those constant assaults and the road became as normal as roads can be in a country at war. I was breathing better.

But was this really me, driving along merrily to meet up with the bastard who'd robbed me of my first real love? Although my broken heart had healed when I married Arsiné, the imprint of my time with Najla still lingers inside me, a shard of unfinished business. Having to deal with the perpetrator of this drama on a day already charged with emotions began scratching the dormant scar. As I was descending into the Bekaa, a lullaby once crooned to the children of the Great Armenian Massacre came on the radio anticipating the imminent Remembrance Day.

> Go, leave this neck of the woods, nightingale
> Stop singing above our roses
> Our souls are dark, our lives bitter
> You're deeply hurting our hearts

Go, tell that you've escaped, nightingale
A country covered in blood
Where rivers flow with tears
And where only the guns prevail.

Is there, I wonder, another people who sing so happily the saddest songs ever? And to make their children sleep? Sure, the Lebanese promise to 'slaughter a dove' for their sleeping babies, but they say it's only a lie to be forgotten when the baby sleeps. The Anglos place the cradle on a tree-top and wait for the wind to break the bough, so down will come baby, cradle and all. But by this time a smart baby would already be asleep.

Years ago, I had a conversation about this with Nader. We'd only just met, were getting to know each other over a beer at the Horse Shoe. Though only a small place on a corner of Hamra Street with a few tables on the sidewalk, the Horse Shoe had the *je ne sais quoi* to draw the sophisticated bourgeois and the weirdoes and literati. At the time, Nader was rolling his own cigarettes from a leather pouch when the arty-farty were tossing their blue Gitane packets on the tables like backgammon dice.

That day, Nader was claiming that most ancient people sing sad songs with joy. He'd once heard a Greek song about how the look in the eyes of a heartbroken lover made the birds die and fall from the trees like autumn leaves, 'and people were dancing and cheering to it.' I said that nowhere else did I get the sense of melancholy and exultation mixed together as in the Armenian songs, mixed in a way that kept them separated; two faces of the same coin, one smiling, the other crying.

As we went through various cultures trying to work out a theory about sad lullabies, Nader's eyes became misty. His gaze drifted away. Then suddenly this guy I hardly knew was singing a song in a foreign language. Everyone hushed, listening to his vision of putting his baby son to sleep in Polish:

34

'Lay down your little head
Let me tell you a fairy tale
There was once a king
And a queen
And a page
They lived among roses
They did not know the storms
Certainly the king loved her
And the page too
They both loved her
And she loved them true
And they all loved each other
But fate was so cruel
They ended up dying
The king was eaten by a dog
The page by a cat
And the queen by a mouse.

'Love, my friends,' Nader concluded, addressing the punters, 'walks hand in hand with death. It's fed to little angels everywhere.'

Cheers and applause. He beamed and saluted everyone.

I hadn't yet discovered, that day, that he didn't merely like an audience, he loved it to the point of debauchery. Cameras, too, were fascinated by this wiry little guy with a face full of features at war with each other: his high brow constantly creased with anxiety, his thin inconsequential nose working overtime to suck oxygen into his asthmatic lungs, and his reedy lips, always dry at the corners, smirking faintly. He combed his silky black hair with his fingers and trimmed his beard only when he remembered that he had one. And he talked, oh how he talked. He could take you to the spring and bring you back thirsty.

Nader had finished law school in Beirut simply to please his mother but then had left for Poland to join the most avant-garde theatre group in the world. He'd learned the language in less than three months and been able to play in Grotowski's productions. At the same time, and despite the gruelling time-table and harsh discipline infamous at that school, he'd managed to learn cinematography while helping his wife Iwona with her own cinema studies. When he landed back in Beirut, he was shocked by the growing civil unrest. He wasn't alone; many young students who'd left a promising Lebanon full of hope came back with the energy and knowledge to be part of its golden years only to find it fermenting with hatred and violence.

But Nader was not deterred. He had plans: a one-man show of Hamlet, and a movie about the Mediterranean as the 'blue pirate' who stole people from its shores and dispersed them around the world. Many people were already leaving, sometimes by boat. So Nader took advantage of the situation to start shooting his Pirate. He invited me to take pictures of the shoot. When I failed to show sufficient enthusiasm, he dangled the carrot: 'Guess who my cameramen are?' I shrugged my shoulders.

'The Baddour brothers!'

I was taken aback. Shooting with the legendary twin camera-men, the best in the Middle East, was tempting. I mean, those guys rolled with people like Schlöndorf and Yousef Chahine. And despite being infamously moody, they could charge an arm and a leg. Were they really working for this guy?

Nader had my advance ready at our next meeting in the Horse Shoe. And he brought along as proof the men themselves: Rero and Reef Baddour, beards and biker jackets and designer sunglasses, moving with the agility of leopards. Hey! Hi! They shook my hand and tapped my shoulder, fulsome in their delight at having me in the crew. We huddled together in a far corner plotting our masterpiece.

The Maestro was over the moon. 'There is thunder in my heart, guys,' he said. 'Thunder. It may kill me before I produce the lightning. That's the only thing that scares me.' He went on to explain his project while we drank blonde beer and white tequila. 'The Mediterranean Sea is the Blue Pirate. It's been pirating us off to other countries for centuries, making it too easy to escape our ordeals. Its pretty waves come towards us like sirens from the depths of history. Those waves are the pirate's mob, coming to lure us away. A few ceremonial farewells and we're elsewhere, other people, our passports a different colour. We're gone forever. Had we been born in a landlocked country, we would have been far more attached to the soil and to each other. Yes, my friends, people are made by their birthplace. And Made in Lebanon is a trademark dissolvable in sea water.'

We all agreed that the idea sounded good but Nader had no script. He had, he said, the inspiration. 'It's a jewel; it glows from within, with a series of illuminations.' And he had 'the big picture', though that could change, too, he added, according to the above mentioned illuminations. He believed that the troubled situation was an open studio; the people were already in their roles. The general lawlessness would give us the chance of some striking shots. Later we'd do a cut and paste. He conceded that his method was unconventional, but far more creative than any framework or style or school. 'The difference between us and Hollywood is that we don't have their means, yet we have the biggest studio under the sun.'

I couldn't tell if the Baddours were buying this spiel or even listening to it. They nodded and smiled but seemed more interested in their tequila. I feared they would drop out in the middle of the shoot and walk away. They'd done it before, to much more serious filmmakers. But maybe they were taken in by Nader's enthusiasm, just like me.

One day we did some shooting around the ancient port of Tyre, Nader managing to convince some of the locals to play a scene – unpaid of course – where they'd bring out their women and children and run along carrying some light luggage as if fleeing their homes. Most of them lived round the corner in the court-yard houses that lined the narrow streets.

But while the locals fell to his charm, the sun kept playing hide and seek with the clouds, preventing the shoot. Prolonged intervals between takes depressed him. It made him fear losing grip on an already volatile situation. He lay down on the quay chain-smoking his hash joints, eyes wide open, waiting for the skies to obey his filming schedule. Meanwhile the Baddours meandered off, mixing with the fishermen at the port.

While we waited, Nader began recounting to me the fall of Tyre and the barbaric crucifixion of all its remaining men at the hands of Alexander the Great. He was relating something that had taken place three thousand years ago as if it had happened yesterday. 'Every boy over twelve is crucified, and all the while Sidon is watching and so is Byblos and so is Beirut. This is our everlasting tragedy, Koko – we never rush to help each other. We'll never become a nation.'

His biggest dream was to film Alexander the Great's siege of Tyre with Toshiro Mifune playing an imaginary Phoenician hero who contradicts history by taking out Alexander. He was infatuated with the protagonist of The Seven Samurai. He said that he adored Mifune so much he would gladly wash his underwear. 'Can you imagine the underwear of a Samurai, Koko?' He smiled to himself, but he was already writing the script and imagining, without a trace of doubt, that Mr Mifune would accept the role. 'We will start with modern times, Koko, interspersed with flashbacks some three hundred years before Christ.'

'I hate flashbacks.'

'Never mind. The film will be called "The Manuscript". It's

about a secret manuscript that tells the true story of Tyre under Alexander's siege. A Lebanese philosophy student called Zeno tracks down a map that shows where the manuscript is hidden.' Nader's hands began shaping the space around him, framing imaginary takes.

I played along with him. 'Maestro, where is the manuscript?'

'In Thessalonica. On the left hand side of a bench on the sea promenade, just in front of the statue of Alexander the Great. OK? So, Zeno boards the train to Thessalonica and takes a taxi from the station to the promenade. It's Sunday. Thousands of people frequent the promenade on Sundays. There's an amorous soldier and his girlfriend making out on the designated bench: a rooster on leave and his little hen nibbling at each other, as if they are extracting gold from each other's teeth.' Nader was watching their virtual courtship already inside their embrace. 'Zeno lurks about. He walks up and down, from one end of the promenade to the other, a hundred times. He buys several cobs of corn, ice cream, baked watermelon seeds, sodas – anything on offer by the street vendors. He even buys a lottery ticket and sits looking at its numbers under the big mounted Alexander, moving into new shade each time the sun hits him. And he talks to the horseman: "I am going to make a joke of you when I find the manuscript, General! I hope that soldier is not sitting here forever; I need the manuscript, General. The whole world needs the manuscript. But most importantly Lebanon. The Lebanese need to know how heroically their ancestors fought to keep you from desecrating their temples and their schools of knowledge. They need to know that had Sidon and Beirut and Byblos risen to help Tyre you would have been history rather than historic". During this monologue we see the women of Tyre handing bucket loads of boiling olive oil to the defenders of the castle and how each drop of that boiling oil is putting Alexander's soldiers out of action. We see Tyre's divers diving to the bottom of the sea and sabotaging the bridge Alexander built from the rubble of the mainland, see it cave in over and over again.'

'Maestro, the amorous soldier could be on leave. He'll be late to the barracks.'

'Yes, yes. Luckily, the lovers never look up to notice Zeno's beady eyes on them. But he can't hate them for being in the wrong place at the wrong time. They are so much in the right place and time for themselves as to make him the intruder. Now Zeno feels his bladder bursting. He turns around the statue facing the sea but as he unzips his fly a boat honks and he whirls around and pees all over the pedestal of the statue – great scene, that!

'Finally,' Nader continued, 'the lovers move away, slowly, still glued to each other, whispering promises, and walk hand in hand into the sunset. Zeno flies like a hungry wasp to their bench. There's a trimmed hedge and a little flower bed on each side. He finds a stick. The soil is damp from recent irrigation. He sits and digs, feigning listless boredom, but his head is filled with troubling scenarios. What if the gardener has found the manuscript while weeding the flower bed and taken it to the authorities and now the dreaded Greek secret police are sitting inside Alexander's horse watching him! Or no – the gardener is a wise guy, he thinks "someone has hidden this manuscript; he'll show up soon and I'll strike a deal with him." But why should he? If he knows how dangerous this manuscript is he will not touch it. He has a family. He has arthritis. Or . . . what if Zeno is on the wrong side of the bench? A couple of hours digging like a mole for nothing? What if there's another statue of Alexander? What if there's a totally different promenade?

'Now Alexander the Great is sinking into darkness and fear is shaking Zeno's patience, threatening his courage. He is just about to give up when the stick breaks. He can't keep his cool any more. He turns his back to Alexander and the few strollers left on the promenade and crouches, digging with both hands.

It's there all right, all damp and muddy, but well packed in flax and double plastic sheets. Two hundred pages of history! He opens the first page and we see Toshiro galloping through the streets of Tyre inciting people to keep up the resistance. Zeno is shaken. He wraps the manuscript in his jacket and hails a taxi. On the train, he reads more. He discovers that Alexander betrayed a deal with the people of Tyre. They'd offered to hand him the keys to the city on the condition that his soldiers refrain from looting the temple. But of course we know what happened. Zeno puts the manuscript back in his jacket, ties it with his shoelaces, makes a pillow of it and guards it with his head all the way back to Athens. He feels greater than Alexander. And he dreams the gates of Tyre are opening and the black horse of the defiant Toshiro is storming out to face that reckless, arrogant Macedonian.'

Nader's face glowed with satisfaction. He loves his endings.

The sun tore through the clouds, dispersing Nader's ramblings together with a flock of pigeons over the port. The languid water rippled with light. The empty boats responded like maidens waking from a deep sleep. I wanted so much to click that precious moment – wings, waves, vessels all baptised with the newborn sun – but Nader popped up like a cork out of a bottle and ran to find the Baddour brothers. I ran after him across the quay to the main entrance. They weren't at the usual café where the fishermen played cards and drank beer and smoked their nargileh, nor by their jeep at the other end of the pier, so Nader sprinted towards the inner maze of old Tyre. He was dying to get on with the next shot. His fear that the sun would again curtail his Pirate was propelling him like a cannonball, but I had three cameras with three extra lenses and films and filter all pounding at my thighs. I couldn't drop them just anywhere. I screamed abuse at Nader, asking him to fucking stop. Shutters clunked open. Heads craned out, loudly voicing their discontent, calling me understandable but undeserving names. Most aggravating those directed to my mother.

'What do you think I'm doing, jogging for exercise?' I yelled back. 'You're all Yes sir, of course sir, when he solicits your help, you're all happy to show your faces in his film, so why don't you catch the bastard before he runs out of breath and drops dead, you morons!'

They were stunned.

At the seafront, we finally saw the Baddours, pants down, squatting on a rock, defecating side by side. Two muscular bohemian twins presenting the blue pirate with two perfect cakes of stool on the same shore where once Princess Elyssa sailed to build Carthage, the Phoenicians discovered how to extract purple dye from murex shells, and Kadmus proudly held up to the world his awesome alphabet plates. Nader was mortified. He was hardly breathing, yet he picked up pebbles and started throwing them at the shitting – now also laughing – twins.

We had to change tactics after that, so Nader hired a small cruiser usually used for short trips between Tyre and Sidon. Our mission was, to put it mildly, hazardous. Day after day we sailed to a central point that covered north and south of the coast. There we waited for the ferry boats carrying refugees away from the growing possibility of war. We would approach them and start a conversation with anyone willing to talk. We might wait all day to spot a boat and even then weren't always lucky. There were endless hurdles. Our skipper drank too much while waiting. He had great difficulty siding the boat close enough to the ferries. The passengers were too seasick to make an effort or show the required enthusiasm of unpaid extras who would never even have the pleasure of seeing Blue Pirate. And there was the sea itself, the splashing of the waves, the risk of the camera getting wet, the rocking, our own seasickness.

Nevertheless, there's nothing more poignant than the truth told from a boat laden with the desperate. 'Don't worry, we have all day,' Nader would call out. 'Tell us, where were you born? How many children . . . how many? Oh my, are they all with you on board? Are they? Great, show them to the camera.' One large hirsute father of four with a large voice to match tossed his toddler in the air before catching him again amongst cries from all over the boat. Even Rero, who held the camera like a mortar launcher and was unflappable, shrieked with horror. 'You see that?' the father cried, 'That one second between air and sea? That's what life's going to be like for those who stay behind.' Then he took his passport out from the inner pocket of his jacket. 'As soon as I replace this cedar tree with a plant that doesn't need blood to stay green, I'll be a happy man.'

I may forget a lot of what I saw later during the war, but not him and the beats my heart missed when he tossed his son in the air.

The twins started discussing different angles for future shots. Reef, the setup artist, suggested climbing on top of the captain's cabin, a slippery two square metres of fibreglass where even the seagulls skidded before finding their balance. Reef was determined. He opened the safety box, extracted a rope, tied the middle of it around his brother's waist, hooked one side to the tiller and asked Rero to climb up barefoot while he went to the bow to find a hook by the cleave for the other end.

'What about his front and back? How will he keep steady?' Nader was pale with worry. Stunts performed by anyone but himself scared him to death.

'Once his feet are in a pre-sprint position, he'll be steady as a rock,' said Reef. 'When we're ready we'll hand him the camera.'

'You mean he's going to stay up there until the next boat comes along?' Nader yelled.

'Nope! We're going to move!' Reef secured the rope and ran

to the skipper's cabin. A minute later we heard him holler, 'Yes, you dickhead, move! We move towards the next boat! Get up or I'll throw you overboard!'

Somehow, Reef got the skipper to sail. Meanwhile Rero was crucified on the cabin's roof, practising balancing with his hands crossed at his chest so he would be able to hold the camera when the time came.

Suddenly Nader yelled, 'What the – Oh my God! This is crazy! Reef, get the camera! Rero, shoot her slow . . . ly, every goddam millimetre of her. Let the camera rest on her, rest with her. Where's the camera? This is my bloody opening shot and I don't – '

Rero fell to his knees. Reef handed him the camera. I had mine ready. Nader was holding his head in his hands and beginning to have an asthma attack, his eyes popping in and out, but he didn't give a fuck. It was a miracle: our first floating cadaver. And it was a young woman, blonde, in a white cotton dress torn at the chest releasing a fair bit of her bosom. Her eyes were open, staring at the universe. She was being rocked in the cradle of the pirate's gang. And because she was moving she seemed to be breathing, and because her eyes were open she seemed to be seeing. Even as I clicked her I shivered. Rero shouted from his watch tower: 'Enough, Koko, don't disturb her.'

Normally, the dead belong somewhere else. When the war finally came, and after my initial shock at the bus massacre, I clicked hundreds of them and always felt the same reaction: You're not here, pal. And more often than not: Wherever you are, it can't be worse than here. It's the living who stirred the most unbearable feelings. Escaping their villages in ramshackle trucks, hunted by helicopters and sniped at from derelict buildings and hilltops. Standing hands-up against walls, awaiting the verdict of a militiaman crazed with vengeance. Trapped under the rubble of a bombed building screaming for help but no one dares while the shelling goes on. And mothers. Especially the mothers. There's a completely different quality to mothers freshly mourning their children. The rock bottom of tragedy stares at you through their eyes, making you wish yours were blind. I wonder if our opening shot had also been a mother.

We were bumping in the waves like a basketball. Nader was wheezing, puffing up and turning blue, his veins about to burst out of his face. A medium-sized yacht was coming straight at us, splitting the waters and leaving in its wake a trail of foam and smoke. 'Skipper!' we howled in panic. Just seconds before it could collide with us, it accelerated abruptly, swerving sideways, sending a tidal wave over our deck. Rero fell off his roof, clutching his precious camera for dear life. The floating woman smacked the side of our boat a few times.

I swear I heard her scream.

The next day the Baddours didn't turn up. It was over. They'd had enough. They left on one of those boats we'd been chasing. News of their journey trickled through in bits via other travellers. From Larnaca they boarded a plane to Paris, where they went looking for work. Next thing we heard was that they'd met the legendary Japanese Siamese twins Niko and Niki who were shooting an episode of their soap opera, a series of sitcoms called "I Am in Love, Not You!" In them, when one of the girls falls in love she wants to disjoin herself from her sister, ready to endure a life-threatening operation, but when her heart is broken she thanks God that she's not alone. In real life Niko and Niki had never been in love until the day they met the Baddours on set. It was love at first sight for all four. But the girls were wary; what if one heart is broken for real? What would they do then? The Baddours, who did everything together anyway, lacking only the glue to become Siamese twins themselves, were so exuberantly uninhibited that they swept the coy Japanese maidens off their feet. We read the story of their wedding in the papers and saw with great merriment one Baddour on each side of the Japanese girls, the grooms in traditional Lebanese dress, the brides in glorious golden kimonos. Every newspaper and magazine in the country republished the picture. It was plastered on bus windows and beauty parlours and walls everywhere. They would have never achieved such fame working for Nader.

As for Nader, he vanished. Rumour had it that he was editing rushes for a TV station in Algiers. Or Niger, and a documentary about the Tuareg. Or Morocco, helping a local filmmaker with her first movie. Naturally, all gossip concerning him came with lashings of salt and pepper. Given his previous debaucheries, he impregnated the Moroccan girl, and her parents chased him across Casablanca. That's how it goes – due to forced isolation and the absence of leisure pursuits during times of civil unrest, the truth recedes, leaving space for wild fabrications. It entertains people to embellish any story, especially one taking place in an exotic kingdom like Morocco or a desert in deepest Africa.

Then he was back in Beirut, but incommunicado.

My stills from Blue Pirate were tucked away in Uncle Varouj's attic. I thought I might write chunky captions for each shot, telling it from a photographer's perspective, have Fathy Nawar edit my broken Arabic and publish them in a book: a testimony of turbulent times by those who opposed the coming war with the weapon of creativity. Fathy agreed to do the editing, but only if Nader would write a preface. 'It's his film after all. Ethically you need his consent.'

I knew where he lived, with his mother in a big colonial apartment in west Beirut. And I had a hunch he'd be there. So I took my chances and knocked at the massive green door. His mother opened up. A tiny woman with challenging eyes, she wore a yellow apron around her waist, her wavy silver hair firmly clamped in a bun. She'd never seen me before, yet she

46

forestalled me with a firm, 'He's not here.' She didn't shut the door in my face but neither did she invite me in. I could smell cooking inside, lots of tomato paste and garlic and cumin. It reminded me of the chick pea and vegetable stew he used to bring in a lunchbox on shoots. I stood and waited, smiling, saying nothing, until her eyes slowly softened. She bowed a little and moved away from the door.

I walked with her down a hallway adorned with classical paintings and oval mirrors. It led to a huge living room, sparsely furnished and dominated by a grand piano. The old woman pointed to the far side and whispered, 'He sits over there, drinking herbal tea and listening to music. Four days now like this.' Then she caught my wrist, pleading, 'Will you make him eat?'

I walked casually towards the recluse. Nader blended with the surroundings, cocooned in a Lazy Boy recliner, wearing silk Bordeaux pyjamas. He looked like a crestfallen lawyer who'd just lost a case.

'Are you in trouble, Maestro?' I said.

'There's only one Maestro here, Koko: Schubert.'

He didn't seem surprised to see me. On the contrary, he spoke in the manner of someone continuing an ongoing discussion: 'I've just been listening to Death and the Maiden, and before that the fourth symphony. You know what that music tells me, Koko? It tells me that there isn't much that can be done now that hasn't been done far better already. Is there ever going to be a novelist better than Tolstoy? A poet better than Shakespeare? A musician better than Beethoven? A filmmaker better than Fellini? Sit back and watch the end of the civilised world, Koko. We are the extras who never featured in the big show. Sit down.'

'I think you are absolutely right, Nader. But work is work and Fathy needs you for a job. He's also worried about you.' I wasn't going to let on that the job in question was for my book.

'Dear old Fathy, he always has a Mission Impossible for me. But I don't, at the moment, feel like moving from this chair, Koko. My bearings are dismantled, all pieces and no screws.'

'I'll tell Fathy you'll be in touch, OK?'

'You can tell Fathy . . . tell him you found me dead. Dead on the floor with blue blood pouring out of me, like that blonde, remember?'

'She was a sleeping angel in that shot. You wouldn't look that good all dead and stinking in a pool of ink. Why don't you get your shit together and rejoin the human race. For better or for worse, we are all you've got.'

'I've got nothing worth getting up for. Nothing.'

'Man, you're not only depressed but depressing. I'm out of here.'

I turned to go.

'Koko?'

'What?'

'Why did you come to see me.'

'Forget it!'

Was the old woman standing there all the time, waiting? She was so tiny she could have been swallowed up by either of the Louis XIV chairs which completed the room's furnishings. She shuffled toward us, constrained by her hunched physique. She held my wrist again, only this time her grip was weaker. '*J'ai du bon cognac pour vous.* It will do you good.' Nader said nothing, just stared at an invisible screen. I followed her. Given the surliness of her *enfant génie*, I felt an urge to humour the old woman.

We sat at a table in the faded but clean kitchen. She brought out a bottle of Napoleon and a large crystal glass. Her hands were surprisingly steady. She poured a generous double for me, then took a small liqueur glass and filled it with a short shot. 'Chin, chin!' she chirped, and gulped down the velvety fire. I took a good swig.

48

We went quiet for a few moments, paying homage to Napoleon.

'Don't mind Nader, he's always been a recluse, from an early age. He had a rough start in life. You see, my dear, he's never seen his father.' She looked at me for effect. I nodded – I'd never seen my father either, not since I was four anyway. She carried on telling me she'd been six months pregnant with Nader when his father left on a boat to Brazil. He never came back. She raised Nader all alone. Her husband kept sending her just enough money to get by, and she had jewellery from her inheritance. She sold everything simply to keep her head high. Never asked, never complained. She gave Nader the best education available in Lebanon. If it weren't for his asthma, she would have sent him to a boarding school in France. He finished school and law school with flying colours, but he never wanted to become a lawyer. He did it for her. He was born an artist. Nothing anyone can do about that. He loved listening to music. She took him with her to the Club Militaire every Wednesday evening. 'In those days, my dear, only the army, and only the higher ranks at that, had the privilege of a small, brilliant orchestra. There were no music schools and concert halls for the general public like today. Other people could only go to The Grand Theatre to hear Oum Kulthoum. But we could go to hear Chopin and Mozart, my dear. It was in the family. My mother loved the great composers. We were in Egypt, Alexandria. Oh, you wouldn't know. Alexandria in those days, my dear, Alexandria . . . ' The old woman drifted away.

'I'm sorry,' I said softly, 'I forgot to ask him to eat. But he looks good. Maybe he needs the break. He doesn't seem to be smoking, which is great, don't you think?'

'Have you ever been to Alexandria?' She was still in Egypt.

'I have to go, Madame, I have work to do.'

'Not before you make him eat. Please. I cooked for him.'

'I know. I can smell the ratatouille.'

'Well then, you must stay and eat with us. Please, Monsieur. What is your name?'

'Krikor. But call me Koko. Everybody does.'

The old woman laughed, showing a perfect set of dentures in a small-jawed mouth.

'Like Coco Chanel. I still have a few of her designs.'

'I'm sorry, but I don't know your name.'

'Eugénie.'

'Well, Madame Eugénie, thank you for your hospitality. The cognac was fantastic. But I really must go.'

'Stay, Koko. Eat with us.' It was Nader. He'd changed into his faded jeans and a thick woollen jumper. His hair was wet. Decades lifted from his mother's face. She pushed her chair back, went straight to the cooker and dished up.

'Did you have to seduce my mother, just to make me eat?' Nader wasn't asking a question or making conversation. He'd just included me in his ghosts. But his mother was delighted – he was eating at long last.

She continued talking about him as if he wasn't there. How he was brought up like a prince. He attended posh Jesuit schools all the way to the college of law. He had private tutors during the summer. His doctor came to check on him at home every week. He occupied three rooms: one sheltered by a couple of leafy gum trees for the summer, one exposed to the morning sun for the winter, plus a study full of his books and records.

I just listened and enjoyed the tasty ratatouille. My childhood and his couldn't have been more different. From school I'd learned only what was essential for my survival. That was enough. At home, I was a spider always weaving my abode in this or that corner of my uncle's one-bedroom apartment. And while Nader was all dressed up to attend concerts at the Club Militaire, I was barefoot, kicking a deflated football in the back streets of Bourj Hammoud. Unlike me he never needed the street. So why, I wondered, had he made it his mission in life to grab what wasn't his? Instead of settling for a law career he reached out to become an actor; instead of then sticking with that he messed around with directing; instead of being satisfied with directing plays, he wanted to be a cinematographer while still fiddling with writing articles and polemics and poetry. So many seeds sown, but none in fertile soil.

But what am I compared to him? What had become of my original dreams? No matter how many weeks or months a click of mine survives the snowball of events, it ends up as wrapping paper for repaired shoes or fish guts. My glories are short lived, no better than those of a street prostitute hitting a fat wallet. I'm less than Nader, I am. He never compromised, never lost the north. He did his thing even if it caused chaos and pain, to himself and others. He followed the unattainable goals of his talent right into shame and scandal. I chose the wider path. True, I have taken a few risks, but I did it cautiously and then scuttled back into the shelter of my natural habitat. I had wanted so much to rise up from the stench of my dark room into the realm of Manoug, have my work exhibited in galleries and hung on lighted walls. And, yes, seeing the works and the rewards of Capa, I'd imagined myself embracing the heroine of Casablanca under the wing of an aeroplane. Whether I had it in me or not, I will never know, but at least Nader tried. He gave it his all.

After the meal we stayed around the table, sipping cognac and listening to Eugénie reminisce about the days of the French mandate and the making of the independence, episodes of past glory when being Lebanese meant being civilised, enlightened and envied throughout the Levant. She was deeply concerned about the rise of confessional rhetoric. 'In my day,' she said, 'it was a mortal sin to speak divisively about religion. Young Muslim and Christian women wore the same clothes, swam and skied and played tennis and learned ballroom dancing and played musical instruments and rode in convertible cars with young men. We were all part of a Mediterranean centre of culture. Diversity was *raison d'être* for us, not a sticking point against modernism and free society.' Then she gripped my wrist with warm, firm fingers. 'Tell me Koko, is it civilised to hate each other over religion? There are days when I am a stranger in my own home. It is better to be deported to a strange land than feel a stranger in your own, huh, Koko? You are Armenian Lebanese. Your family must have gone through hell before landing here. But now you are one of us. What do you think? Will Israel succeed in dividing Lebanon, make us all small and turned against each other? I hope to die before it happens.'

We were half way through the Napoleon bottle when Nader's mood mellowed. He was willing to come with me to meet Fathy after all.

'You must come back soon, Koko,' Eugénie said, holding my hand tight as she walked us to the door and down the steps all the way to the street. Perhaps she needed to see for herself her son finally rejoining the human race. A thin frail old woman, incongruous in her dressing gown and tatty apron, waving us goodbye. I didn't know it then, but that was my last sight of her.

Nader had had one Napoleon too many. I gripped his arm in mine to steady him. Surprisingly, he didn't react. An auspicious moment; normally Nader hated to be touched. He couldn't stand the way men kiss and hug each other in our part of the world, yet we hit the street arm in arm, like old buddies.

'Nader,' I said. 'I've been thinking. If I make a book out of my Pirate stills, will you write a preface for it?'

He stopped and stared at me. 'Koko, the Pirate isn't finished. I want to finish it. So don't write its obituary until it's dead, OK?'

'But –'

'No buts on this one, Koko.'

'My shots are mine, Nader. I can publish the book without your damn introduction.'

'After we finish. We could have the book at the opening.'

'You'll never finish anything in your life.'

'You don't know how determined I am. You have no idea.'

'You have no camera. You have no crew. You have no friends, remember? And now you have no Koko, remember that.' I left him in the middle of the road and walked away.

Hearing what happened, Fathy found a solution: 'You were on assignment from the *Daily Sun* when you shot those pictures. the *Daily Sun* have all the rights to publish them under any form it chooses. It will simply be done under our own auspices.'

'Why didn't we do it this way in the first place?'

'I thought an introduction by Nader would be best.'

We sat and chose the photos together. I wanted the floating woman on the cover, but Fathy said no: 'It's too much in the reader's face. Besides, death isn't commercially attractive.' We settled for a shot from the old port of Tyre: the long jetty thrusting deep into the blue pirate with an escapee's boat leaving the port. 'The long quay is a dead end; after it is empty space, like the future of those people. Ending and beginning together,' said Fathy.

I expected Nader to object. Even feared him showing up at the launch and making a scene, but he didn't.

Then one day I heard that he backed up his car and ran over his mother while she was rushing after him with food for the road. Someone said everybody was having problems with the gear-shift of the new Renault 6. But why would he change gears at the door of his own garage if he'd just taken off? It didn't make sense. No one saw the actual accident. A neighbour mentioned that Nader had left the house in great haste, but that was nothing unusual. A passer-by saw him getting out of the car, collapsing with shock after the accident and howling. That drew the street's attention. The police report saw nothing more than tragic human error. They detained him overnight and released him without charges.

Poor little Eugénie. I'd liked her thin, vibrant frame, her piercingly emotional eyes, her unconditional devotion to her wayward son. She looked so tiny in that big house and yet she filled it with warmth and caring. The way she died, crushed by a car like my parents, made me hate Nader more than ever. Unconsciously I superimposed his face onto that of the driver who'd killed my parents. I didn't want to go to the funeral, I wanted to avoid him. But the boss insisted. Even if Nader was only an occasional contributor, 'His name appears in our pages, he writes for us,' said Burhan Sadik. 'Come with me, and Fathy will meet us there.'

People were lined up at the church entrance to pay their condolences. Nader wore a grey oversized jacket from the fifties most probably left behind by his father. No necktie. He had a sheepish smile on his face, shaking hands with commiserates as if he were receiving congratulations. He was oblivious to the wicked speculations whispered around him (money, inheritance, life insurance . . .), purveying a sense of submission to destiny: Shit happens, there is nothing we can do about it. I wasn't so sure. I brooded on his recklessness, his fiery temper and his constant drifts from reality. He was probably so self-absorbed that day that he hadn't bothered to look in the rear-view mirror. I couldn't make myself shake his hand. I just walked into the church and placed a white rose on Eugenie's casket.

After that, our paths should never have crossed again. But destiny had given him a further fateful mission: causing my first and worst heartbreak.

5

It all started with a work assignment: 'Find Najla Helou, the painter who also poses for students. There are rumours she's preparing a scandalous exhibition. But be warned – she's elusive.' I still have that note hidden in one of my film cartridges. I still have the negatives of our first encounter, still sometimes long for Najla despite my happiness with Arsiné and Nishan. To be more precise, I long for the dream-like days and nights we had together.

Fathy didn't want a reporter on that job. He had given me a tape recorder and a few questions to ask her and told me to keep the matter from the scribes: 'A smartass is the last thing we need on this one. They could blow it. Bring me the quotes and I'll write the story.' What story? Beirut's all-powerful archbishop had called Fathy to say that 'trustworthy sources' claimed Najla was preparing an exhibition entitled When Mary Was Pregnant with Him. The paintings, said the archbishop, could incite a violent reaction from Christian zealots. Better to nip the project in the bud. So I was sent to spy on Najla Helou under the guise of an innocent arts interview.

Until then my carnal life had consisted of easily quenched and quickly forgotten desires, no changes in chemistry worth mentioning. Not until Najla opened the door to me that fateful afternoon. I meant to say the standard, 'Krikor Krikorian from the *Daily Sun*' (she was expecting me), but I was struck dumb by a sudden warm quiver in my groin. I'd never felt anything like it before, nothing that overwhelmed my whole being like this did.

She smiled and tilted her head a fraction, swiftly sizing me up. 'Come on in, Koko.'

Her seventh-floor Raouché apartment was filled with a soft pre-twilight translucence that served me well. I hid my troubled face behind the lens, reciting the few questions I'd memorised from Fathy's note, and clicked away, fifty or sixty shots of her, her studio and her paintings. She moved between her canvases, alternately showing and telling: 'You can't understand the journey of a model if you don't live it. And once you do, you start painting with a completely different rhythm, from a totally different angle. Imagine Van Gogh painting The Potato Eaters after just a weekend in their homes. Impossible. I don't paint 'from' life; I paint life itself, from the inside out,' she said. My breathing was following the waves of her body under her loose silk dishdasha like a hungry seagull. Her halo of curly red hair, her pronounced upper lip, her sleep-starved slanted eyes, and her skin – silk and cotton woven to an ivory polish – each aspect of her beauty was blowing me in a different direction.

She was clear with her words, carefree in her attitude. She must have suspected I was hunting for scandal but she allowed me free access to all the paintings stacked against the walls. There were lots of women in different shapes and forms, but none of them was either Mary or pregnant. Most of her work was impressionist/surrealist: nothing is as it seems, inciting bewilderment akin to meeting someone you think you know but can't place the name or the context. So you look deep into the face searching for an answer. The fact that you never get the answer is beside the point, because not only is your memory stirred but your imagination, too, is rushing to the fore, which takes you to your own interpretation of the painting. And that's what really matters.

The talk about Najla was that she had lovers but never a partner. Her highly respectable family had more or less dis-owned her. She was living her own life, as a modern woman in modern times. And she was notorious for breaking the rules. A few years before, she'd turned her house into a literary salon where poets and artists congregated to read, perform music and discuss the politics of change. An open house belonging to a single bohemian woman was bound to become a source of seedy speculation. The vice squad stormed it and carted everyone off to the infamous Hbeysh police station, where the women were treated as prostitutes and the men as adulterers. Fortunately, one guest was a prominent French playwright being feted by the Lebanese government. The French Embassy intervened, prompting a quick end to the case. Nonetheless, after the raid Najla shut her doors and disappeared from circulation for a long while. Then she began exhibiting quietly in small galleries, trying to avoid adverse exposure.

When we sat in her bamboo-furnished living space, Najla gently removed the camera from my hand, like pulling a toy from a sleepy child. 'A couple of weeks ago,' she began, confirming that she'd read my covert mission, 'I was with some friends when someone complained that nothing exciting was happening in the Beirut art scene nowadays. We started playing around with ideas just for fun. An image of the Madonna nine months pregnant standing at dusk on Mount Olive was just one of them, probably not even mine. How it trickled through the city gossip to become An Exhibition by Najla Helou, I don't know.' Najla cupped her temples with her hands. 'If only I could understand this hostility.' Then all of a sudden she said, leaning over and pulling her dishdasha up to her knees : 'Look at my feet, Koko, they're as white as two bottles of milk. You know why? Because I stopped going to the beach. And you know why? Because every female in this country can wear a bikini except Najla Helou. Even if I swam in a Chador it would become a scandal. So, when I can afford it I go somewhere like Cyprus where I can be a naked nobody in peace.'

The one truth in her reputation was that she did indeed believe monogamy was hypocrisy and marriage a silver coffin for cowards. 'A recipe for slaying passion,' she said. 'I am an artist, a maker of new forms. I can only do that in complete freedom, leaving all the doors of my life open, including my emotions and my body.'

When, a little later, I got up to go, Najla put her hand softly on the back of my head.

'Won't you stay for a drink, Koko?'

But I couldn't trust myself to linger any longer. 'Maybe when I bring you the contact sheets?'

'Tomorrow?'

'Day after tomorrow.'

'Seven, seven-thirty.'

I was there at seven on the dot. I'd tried to delay my arrival until seven-fifteen – correct but not too hasty – but I just couldn't. While in the taxi, I'd stuck my head out of the window and looked up. Her studio was flooded with light. By contrast, the balcony twinkled with tiny electric candles tucked among the flower pots. The whole floor looked like a space station, making me an astronaut in a troubled orbit.

I didn't feel the elevator lifting off up to her floor.

She opened the door immediately and gave me a lingering kiss on the cheek.

I'd always been dubious about women wearing jeans for an evening rendezvous; it meant at best, later. Whereas a skirt or a flowing dress was more neutral, perhaps inviting. But the jeans Najla wore that night were softened by the loose white silk top that was fluttering against her breasts like the hands of a mime artist in a shadow theatre.

We looked at the contact sheets. She said she liked them all and praised my eye.

I asked her to choose her favourites just in case the page makers decided on one she didn't approve of. She laughed: 'Let them surprise me. I like surprises.'

We had a few drinks on the balcony overlooking Beirut's bay

of love and suicide. Colour was everywhere around us, waves of colour, on canvas, in cushions, the curtains, the pots, the tablecloth. The night that domed the sea before us was lit with trillions of promising stars. We joked about the archbishop and his seedy suspicions, though I for one was grateful he'd brought us together.

The vodka martinis were throwing me back into teenage ambivalence: physically ready, mentally inept. What my imagination had woven during the last couple of days unravelled. Not one good line came to my lips. Finally I played all my cards in one suicidal hand: 'I haven't had much sleep the last two nights,' I said, looking Najla straight in the eye. 'I've been thinking about you like a zombie with an arrow in his forehead. And now I can't bear you with your clothes on.'

Then I took her in my arms.

That first kiss saw the night into dawn.

People talk about love at first sight, but love was too average a concept measured against our stormy passion. I loved her to the point of effacement. I just melted away in her shadow, quickly learning her little quirks, moulding myself to meet them. Like her need for absolute silence to begin each day. She'd wake up, turn on to her belly and lean over the edge of the bed contemplating the floor. She'd look at it silently for a while. Any noise, no matter how small, would annoy her. 'Those few moments are like the pause of a newborn before it emits its first scream for oxygen. I need to feel brand new every time I wake up to the world. You know what I mean, Koko?'

Koko knew nothing except that he was happy beyond the limits of happiness.

I served her breakfast in bed and sat watching her nibble her croissant and sip hot chocolate while she examined her sketches from the previous night. She threw nothing away. 'You never know when a discarded sketch might yell, Don't leave me to die! Paint me!'

I didn't care what the critics said about her technique, all the mumbo jumbo about her 'unrefined approach to paint'. None of those failed painters and frustrated teachers-turned-critic had ever lost themselves before canvas, unable to eat or drink, completely tranced inside the motion of every brush stroke and every surge of inspiration. I saw her losing weight by the hour. I saw her limbs shiver and shake. I saw her eyes explode with joy and dim with despair. I saw her crushed by defeat and lifted in ecstasy. I enjoyed seeing her working, the way she kept tilting further and further to one side until she was standing on one leg like a swan about to take off. And I trembled with her seismic orgasms when she was finished painting and we made love on the studio floor. Even then there was a river of colour in her eyes.

Sure, we weren't 'compatible'. I wasn't commenting on her paintings or discussing Foucault with her. But I listened to her with all the patience of an idolater, weathering her attacks of fury and her brooding over artist's block. And I was there when she was ill. I made her soup and brought her a bucket to vomit in. I wiped her mouth and held her in my arms for hours. I endured happily her interminable whingeing about how artists should be spared physical ailments because 'we live outside our bodies. Illness makes me feel like an illegal immigrant caught by the border guards.' Then, the minute her temperature dropped and she was able to hold a brush again, she'd forget all about it.

During the next two months I took an assignment out of my league simply because it made it possible for us to be together. The *Daily Sun* was running a series of articles about the forgotten Roman ruins scattered all over Lebanon. There were many, some small, others quite remarkable, mostly on hilltops. So we bought a tent and camping gear and drove off in pursuit of the ancient Romans. We camped outside villages tucked in wayward valleys near crystal-clear springs. We gathered wood for fire, baked potatoes and acorns and drank arak and made love deeply, cushioned in the arms of mother earth. Najla seemed to have found her element. She remained near-naked all the while we were alone in the woods, eating and drawing and sleeping with nothing on but a flimsy little shift. Sex in the open air was her deliverance, her exit from blockage and despair. And it made her laugh. 'How many loaves did you put in the oven, darling?' Still quivering with excitement after making love, she would giggle and cite that line from a story by Balzac about an innocent bride who boasts that her groom is 'king of grooms' and had put twenty-four loaves in the oven on their wedding night while in reality she was still a virgin.

In the mornings Najla went to the neighbouring farms looking for young girls to pose for her among the ruins. 'They're like Greek maidens from antiquity', she said. 'I'll paint them flying like birds outside time and space.'

We squandered time without a thought. We were into each other so perfectly it felt as if each of us had created the other from nothing. 'You're becoming a painting I'll never be able to relinquish, Koko,' she said. 'If I say that I love you I may die; and I am dying to say it.'

6

Coming back to 'civilisation' was inevitably a downer. We resumed city life like jet-lagged passengers dumped in a foreign land. Najla became restless. She'd stored up heaps of energy and pencilled hundreds of sketches, yet she couldn't stay in-doors and paint, as what we'd learned from the land and its people fuelled our revolt against the current situation. There was innocence out there, good God-fearing simple honest people who did not deserve to be dragged into the growing mire of factional squabbles and hatred. We craved action. The turpitude of the weary and the defeated irritated us. A civil war was beginning to look more and more likely. We talked about it among friends in cafés, we attended rallies, we organised discussions. Najla even came out of her seclusion to do a TV interview; dressed in fatigues, she attacked the political system with biting sarcasm, calling the politicians rats and cockroaches.

Think-alike men and women met up most often at the Smugglers Inn, a stone's throw from the American University. We gathered with them in this stifling den where the tables were squashed together and everyone heard everyone else and commented and argued with everyone about the good of the nation. Smugglers was run by Georges Zeenny, a tall green-eyed dandy whose fame stretched even to the Lebanese Diaspora. But in Beirut he was a legend. 'Have you been Georged today?' Exposure to him, like being caught in bed with Lolita, was a hard habit to kick.

As we entered the cottage-like inn one evening, Georges cat-walked towards us with extended arms, his divine smile dwarfing his beaky nose. 'Just in the nick of time! How extraordinary! I was just going to call you!' Najla nudged me – baloney. But I waltzed into Georges' embrace: 'Just checking on you, gorgeous. We won't stay long.'

'Armenians! Always in a hurry!' He turned and shouted towards the kitchen, 'Ya batal!' (Everyone who worked for him was 'hero'.) A young waiter poked his head out of the hatch. 'Bring my bottle over here.' Then Georges looked tenderly at Najla, 'How is our genius?'

Najla muttered something inaudible. Her current bout of artist's block had put her in a bad mood. We sat at Georges' special table. The batal brought a pretty carafe of cognac together with three crystal glasses.

Naturally, Georges had a new project afoot, an exhibition called 'Postcards From Beirut.' What did we think of the title? He spread across the next table some fifty postcards depicting Beirut's evolution since the dawn of photography, some in sepia and black and white, others in glossy colour.

Najla was readily dismissive. 'What exactly is the message here?'

'Ah, the message! As usual, *ma chérie*, I am the message and the messenger. But for the general public, this is about the imminent end of a six-thousand-year-old city. The end of the cultural centre of the Levant. The end of the avant-garde bridge between east and west. Beirut as we know it will be disembowelled and thrown to the dogs. Worse even than the seven earthquakes that buried it before and after the Romans. The cosmopolitan jewel of the Mediterranean is finito, my friends. There is a conspiracy – I know this for a fact, I have my sources as you know – Beirut is slated to become a bordello for the Gulf States and an international centre of money laundering. It makes me cry. Oh yes, these postcards represent my tears. They are saying to you that Georges Zeenny has begun his mourning of Beirut. But you know me, I have to cry with style.' His eyes were as tearful as those of an obsessed tailor gathering rags to make a pretty garment. 'Have another shot. It's Metaxa, a good Greek brandy. I put it in this lovely bottle to trick myself into a posh mood. How's life behind the lens, Koko?'

After a few minutes of pleasantries, Georges returned to his postcards, determined not to be sidetracked. Determined, too, to involve us. Gradually the mood changed until finally Najla dropped her reservations and jumped into the think tank: 'How about enlarging a few of the postcards and billboarding them to advertise the show?'

'Don't even think of giant enlargements,' I said. 'Double poster size maximum. Otherwise we'd have to use printing and paste pieces which are cumbersome and fragile.'

But Georges wasn't happy with any of it. He imagined hooligans taking a piss at his babies and shooting or defacing them with graffiti. No, he wanted to advertise it through the media as always. 'They're here every night. I feed them fattoush and listen to their bullshit. They'll do their work for me like the good boys they are. And I'll print a book, like an album. One day people will show it to their children, tell them, "This was the city of our childhood, here were the souks, the cinemas, the theatres, the book shops, the traditional cafés, the craftsmen . . . No, my child, Beirut was not only food and fuck. It was a real metropolis." You want message, my princess? There you go.'

What's more, his conspiracy theory was beginning to sound coherent, even plausible, with the rise of his passion, a passion supported by his 'sources'. Secret Service personnel were also punters at Smugglers. He eavesdropped on their discussions and phone calls. In the absence of genuine information, Georges was our fifth column. He was sure, for example, that unauthorised archaeologists were planning clandestine digs in some areas of Beirut's centre to steal the treasures and use the coming war to cover their own traces against future excavations. Worse still, Georges believed that well-connected businessmen were planning to finance specific militias to blow up specific buildings and keep the heat high in Beirut.

A few more Metaxas later, we arranged the postcards in groups. A dozen sepias depicting Beirut's golden years as a centre of commercial activity: cargo ships at the port, horse carriages, women in vaulted souks, street sellers, whores on balconies, the fish market, unloading vegetables from mules and donkeys. In black and white, the cultural side with mosques and churches and universities and reproductions of engravings by Orientalists. In colour, leisure: the hotels by the sea, the restaurants and cafés, the Corniche, the famous water-skiers. Each one was meticulously positioned and carefully contemplated as if we were communing with spirits. After a systematic numbering of each postcard, we swigged the last drop of Metaxa, clinking glasses.

But the ball kept rolling, and soon a whole pre-war antiwar festival was born. A High Cry Against Violence, said the head-lines. Najla produced her females flying through dark magenta with arms crossed like praying angels. 'Her best work ever,' wrote the same critic who once branded her 'a disgrace to the brush'. That was a delicious moment, seeing him nodding as he contemplated the paintings hung on a street wall.

Georges had got everyone on side. The gendarmerie, the army, the different factions, the political parties – he solicited the cooperation of them all. And of course the residents of the street themselves; he had to convince them to park their cars some-where else for the day. Amazingly, they all agreed, as if Georges' charm included car insurance when every other insurance had ceased to function. Najla and I worked with the artists and the craftsmen organising the stalls of home-made produce, artefacts and bric-à-brac. Painters brought their easels. Sculptors chiselled and carved away in an ad hoc symposium. Jazz musicians filled the air with their trumpets and saxophones, while children painted flowers and tanks. A roaming mime performer dazzled everyone with his struggle to break away from an imaginary prison. Georges' postcards were printed on canvas and raised on poles like flags. Prizes were won, courtesy of Beiruti merchants. A butcher decorated a freshly-slain lamb with the colours of the national flag and fed it free of charge to the crowd.

I was jubilant, but the next day Najla woke up on the wrong side of the bed. Instead of looking down at the floor as usual she was staring blankly at the ceiling.

'What's the matter, darling?'

'We did it for ourselves, Koko, for our own egos. The storm didn't go away, nor is the port any nearer today.'

'Well, we did light a candle, as the saying goes, didn't we?'

'We lit a candle and cursed the darkness even more. The flame was too small, the wind will blow it out too quickly for others to see.'

'I don't understand you. We worked. We touched lives. We made a point. What more do you want?'

'Nothing. I just want to be alone.'

'You're never satisfied. Why don't you try to work? Once you start painting you'll be fine. Look at you.'

'Don't. I hate you when you say that with your mouth twisted like that. Oh, just fuck off.'

So I fucked off. I wasn't angry, just frustrated. How could she imagine that one day of peace, love, and culture was going to halt the general deterioration of the country? People everywhere want to live in peace, yet everywhere every mother's son is cradling a gun. You do what you can to express your revulsion at the state of things, and you may as well enjoy your work while it lasts. It seemed to me that Najla allowed her vanity to override her reason, making her believe that she could change the world with a flick of her fingers. It wasn't enough that she might make just a little temporary change. She'd been so high on illusion that her disillusion brought her down with a crash. Maybe, too, she couldn't bear me seeing her crushed vanity.

A few days later she called, all stirred up about a trivial matter not even remotely related to our rift. 'A wasp is nesting above my bedroom window. I can't work. Get your Armenian ass over here!' This was one of many translations of Sorry, I've been a bitch.

And so once again I plunged back onto that rollercoaster called Life With Najla.

Chez Tony was another hangout we visited, when we needed to get out of Beirut. A converted fisherman's shack overlooking a rocky beach north of Byblos, it served fresh fish, home-brewed arak, and thin bread baked by Tony's mother. The place held about twenty bohemians in its communal spirit, all drinking and smoking and singing and dancing and flirting together as the waves stroked the Mediterranean's flanks below us.

Then one evening Nader was there. He stood up and sang his sad Polish song. No one understood a word, but his intense immersion in it brought tears to many eyes. Including Najla's. At that moment, the groin quiver of my first meeting with her recoiled like a frightened crab. The second it happened I knew that Najla was gone, though on another level I refused to believe it.

In no time at all, Najla and Nader were drawn together into an animated tête-a-tête. They were discussing his proposed one-man show of Hamlet, tossing around ideas for the stage set: all-black background, all-white, black and white, a splash of red, better still a mural depicting the major scenes – maybe working together, she paints while he rehearses, hey, we could even take the show to the Yerevan Shakespeare Festival, you know the one, where they do one-man-shows based on works by the Bard?

Two intellectual wankers rubbing shoulders under my jealous nose, talking about Armenia, my genetic homeland, forgetting I was even there. I felt the heat rising in my guts. It must have shown, for bearded-gentle-giant Tony put on an Armenian record and began jigging to the music as if to voodoo away the evil spirit. I'd been drinking neat shots of Vodka. Hot blood flooded my brain. I pulled Najla up to dance the titillating Tamzara. Although it can be performed in several ways, I chose the macho version, inviting a second beautiful woman from the punters. I spread my wings across both women's shoulders and stomped away, pounding the floor so hard it groaned under my boots. Najla learned the steps quickly and danced wholeheartedly with me, but I could sense that part of her was still at Nader's table. The other woman was gazing at me with gratifying admiration. I could read her fingers on my shoulder, feel her hip nudging softly at mine, but her message was lost on me. I was sweating cold, then hot, then dizzy, feeling the anchor of my journey with Najla sinking to the bottom and crumbling into rust.

And so it was that Nader Abi Nader invaded our nest. At the beginning he'd come to the apartment for afternoon tea to discuss Najla's sketches for his Hamlet. It didn't seem to bother either of them that I was always there. I even made tea and joined in the bullshit. Then the project moved to the rehearsal studio. I drove Najla there and back every time. Najla never showed the slightest hint of nuisance at my constant presence. On the contrary, she was more loving than ever. Working chased out her demons. She became tame and tender.

One day I left Nader and Najla working in the rehearsal studio and vaguely registered that he had just started reading a book about the different actors who'd played the role of Hamlet. I happened to notice the page he was on; it had a striking picture of Sarah Bernhardt, probably the only woman ever to play the role. Najla was some distance away, painting a detail on the set. Three hours later, I came back. Nader was still sitting in the same place, reading the same page, his chest pulsing and his eyes sinking in their sockets. It was impossible for him to read nothing for all that time. I threw out a casual bait: 'So, what have you two been doing?'

'Reading,' said Nader, a little too quickly. Najla just smiled her sweeter-than-joy smile and came down the ladder all sweaty to give me an anaesthetic hug. I took it. But later that evening I picked the book up and skipped through it. Guilgud was pointing at the skull like a teacher dismayed by the slackness of his pupil. Barrymore, the best Hamlet according to Orson Welles, scowled at another skull as if looking in a mirror. Sir Lawrence Olivier was about to launch into his whingeing To be or not to be. Cold, coarse Alec Guinness with his thin goatee and bedroom eyes seemed moulded of silver wax. The notorious drunk, Richard Burton – I'd seen his Hamlet on TV, all twentieth-century clothes and a lot of jumping on tables and chairs. None of them had a single line of comment from Nader. Had he read, he would have left scribbles all over the pages. But no, they were neat, untouched. Reading he was not.

Still I said nothing, did nothing. I dithered in my doubts and denials for weeks, until after the performance, when I said that I was going to Bourj Hammoud for the night to see why Arsiné (still my best friend) hadn't made it to the show. But my car broke down, and by the time I got it fixed it was too late to bother her, so I drove back to Raouché . . . and to Nader's little post-production celebration. For Nader's ego had been so puffed up by that evening's applause that he had found the guts to come to Najla's apartment and jump into my bed with her.

I can still see him, standing naked at the door, covering his dick with one of her paintings, his neck protruding like a slimy turtle's: 'Don't disturb us, Koko, we're communing with each other.'

I pushed past him and barged into the apartment shouting, 'I'm going to break your backbone and kill this traitor!' Najla had locked herself in the bathroom. I threatened to break down the door, while somewhere behind me Nader grabbed his clothes and tumbled down the stairs.

'No violence, Koko. Please,' Najla whimpered.

'Then open up!'

'I don't want you to see me like this,' she sobbed.

'Do you love that scum bag?'

'Love has nothing to do with it, Koko.'

'Then what is it?'

'It's about being desperately needed by someone you admire. And if you must know, if it pleases your male ego, mostly he just sleeps in my arms like a child.'

She also told me, in that weird confession, that nothing had happened between them until recently when Nader was trying a physical stunt and fell flat on his back. She thought he'd broken something and rushed to help him. 'He was looking at me like a man drowning in mud.' Just a hug. A bit of tenderness. After all, we're all friends, we're all artists: emotional, sensual. Nothing wrong with a hand stroking the back of someone's head and then –

'Fuck the both of you!' I punched the bathroom door hard and left, cursing in my mother tongue.

7

Nothing had prepared me for being dumped by my first true love. What followed was like a junkie's cold turkey. Unbearable insomnia fuelled my imagination with murderous scenarios. Killing Nader ballooned from a psychological escape to an obsession that gained momentum night after sleepless night. Walking down a street, I would break out in manic laughter at the imagined fruition of a scheme that would annihilate him. I stab him repeatedly in a delicious frenzy. I stalk him all the way to Clemenceau and shoot him in a back alley. I fist-punch him until his face becomes a crushed tomato. Oddly enough I never imagined myself harming Najla. I roamed the streets, losing my way in the most familiar neighbourhoods. Alcohol, pot, sleeping pills – nothing lifted the siege of gloom that permeated my spirit. I wanted Najla back at any price, back to the time of our idyll, to those heavenly months in the countryside when we celebrated beauty and love every morning, every night, every moment.

Throughout that period I couldn't show my face in Bourj Hammoud. I stayed with Emile. He made excuses for me at work and tried hard to cure me of Najla. He even fixed me up with a nymphet he promised would rattle my balls and make me forget I'd ever met 'that bitch'. Meet Pascale: a sexy, slick bourgeoise who drove a Ferrari convertible as red as sin and wore a fifty-thousand-dollar diamond anklet. She invited me to her villa for 'a relaxing evening', with drinks and dinner served by two discreet Philippinas who moved like shadows. Oysters, crab, Russian caviar, French white wine and a mountain of exotic fruits. The swimming pool looked like an extension of the sea. It rippled in yellow and green lights across the dining room's glass door. Soft jazz seeped from the walls and intertwined with the musky scent of fresh flowers.

Emile must have sketched my manhood out of all proportion, for Pascale's eyes began undressing me even before we moved to her dimly lit salon d'hiver. She kept asking why I was so sad. Did I need money? Would I like to take a shower? Use her magic massage recliner and then slip into the jacuzzi? Take a dip in the swimming pool? – it's heated and very sensual. The more she wooed me the more I was seeing the easy pleasures ahead as a hurdle rather than a treat. Sure, part of me was craving sex. At one stage, while listening to Nat King Cole and sipping a warm Armaniac, I wished Pascale would pillage me, shred me to bits. But most of me was desperately longing for Najla.

Finally I just took off, leaving Emile's present unwrapped.

The next day I went home.

Uncle Varouj tried to shake me up roughly: 'It's your own fault,' he said. 'The minute you suspected betrayal, you should have lifted your head up, up, for God's sake, and walked away. Never ever do that again. Women are not goddesses.' And 'When a woman fucks a man and dumps him, she reigns over his vanity the way a castrator reigns over his eunuch.' And more gently, 'Let her go, Krikor, let him have her. It's for the best, son. She was good for adventure, not for life. For life you need a rock, not a high wave. You've had your surf. Now leave the water behind, step onto firm ground. And don't look back.'

Aunty Clauda wasn't so naïve as to try healing me with herbs and good home cooking. Yet she did all that, pursing her lips and mumbling to herself. Her words were inaudible, but I knew all the old sayings anyway: Take from your own, your own will honour you. Jump higher than you can reach and you'll break your neck. Men who fall for loose women are fools to the end. They all said the same thing: Don't cross to the other side lest you be lost. But it was too late for old wisdom to make a difference. I knew she was right, yet right had never seemed so wrong to me. Besides, when have wise words ever cured a broken heart? My reasoning and my resolve were disconnected. I had my meals with Uncle Varouj and Aunty Clauda by the window and tried to reconnect with the hubbub of the street while listening to stories about broken water pipes and stolen electricity lines. A heavy mist engulfed me. I was trapped inside it. At night, I relived all my memories and revisited every detail of my time with Najla, looking for the gaps that had permitted Nader to infiltrate my turf.

Only Arsiné was a comfort. On seeing me at her door she gasped in horror, 'Oh, my dear Koko, what has she done to you?' And she took me so firmly in her arms I didn't want her ever to let go. Unlike my uncle, she believed that I should sort out my relationship with Najla. 'Put your pride on hold, go to her and see if you still have a future together. If she says no, then the wheel has fallen, Koko. You have to stop running.' She said that no one in their right mind would spurn a worshipper like me.

Arsiné had been so impressed by my relationship with Najla. She'd viewed me with wonder and pride. 'You conquered Mount Everest!' she once laughed. Did she suspect, deep down, that it was nothing but surf-riding, that no matter how high it went, it was bound to crash sooner or later? But as long as I was happy, she never said a bad word about Najla.

Or about Nader. Arsiné had come with me to one of his Hamlet rehearsals. She'd sat in a dark corner making herself invisible lest the Maestro rant. Najla was painting the decor while he was talking to himself, directing himself, arguing with himself. 'Hamlet is the state of mind we're in today, remember that. It's a play in a play in a play like Russian dolls. You're all the characters and yourself at the same time. I am Fortinbras and Ophelia, I am the ghost roaming your dark souls . . . ' And then he started digging, jabbing the cement floor with a crowbar until he was drenched in sweat and had 'found' the skull. 'That skull had a tongue in it, and could sing once; how the knave jowls it to the ground, as if it were Cain's jaw-bone, that did the first murder!' He must have shaken Arsiné – she sneaked out without saying a word.

Nonetheless, she later insisted on attending his ridiculous lecture at the Arab University: "Was Shakespeare a Sufi?" Nader was high as a kite, of course. He flung his arms out and cried, 'Alas, poor world, what treasure hast thou lost.' According to him, there was good reason to believe that the bard's name was in reality Shaykh al-Sabir, a Moorish ambassador who'd come to London and signed his plays with the pseudonym 'Shakespeare'. Arsiné had to stifle her laughter during his ranting, but still, she wouldn't say a word against him, only 'He's just an odd painting in a shabby frame at the wrong exhibition.'

Now Arsiné was all afire to show me the graduation project for her degree in design. Perhaps, too, she hoped to distract me from my misery. 'Close your eyes,' she said, walking me towards her room. 'Now when I say open, open!'

I looked, amazed. 'What's this?'

'A picture made entirely of dried wildflowers. I've been keeping them since we were kids. You like?'

I was speechless. I remembered her picking flowers wherever we went but had no idea they would end up going with her to university. I moved closer to the hanging canvas. The dried flowers were still glowing. I looked at her, raising my eyebrows.

'It's a special spray-glue. Very delicate.'

'A whole springtime, captured one tiny piece at a time,' I marvelled.

'You'd never guess that was two years of hard work, Koko. What do you think?'

What's more, she'd researched every one of those wildflowers, copied both their Latin and local names in an index to the project, and written an introduction. The pressing, drying and conserving demanded meticulous attention. Sometimes a neck would break, she said, or petals fall at the slightest touch. 'Like butterfly wings, but flimsier. I had to hold my breath with each one until it was safely pasted.'

We had a pot of coffee and reminisced about picking flowers, falling from trees, playing soccer and getting into brawls. Arsiné never turned her back on a brawl. She was lean but had strong limbs, and she used them like a kick boxer. She wouldn't bite unless someone locked her neck, but once she bit a guy and I remembered him screaming, 'Aren't they feeding you at home?'

'You still remember that!'

'You almost ate the bugger.'

Having grown up together on the same street had given us an affection and confidence in each other and a bond that was rock solid. Arsiné never changed. Even the neat boyish bob she'd chosen in her early teens remains the same to this day.

There were moments, while we talked that day, when her eyes welled with the intensity of her concern. And moments when I asked myself why we weren't together, given how close we'd always been. But things between us didn't move in that direction, couldn't yet, not until I'd reached the end of my obsession with Najla.

That end came one Wednesday. Late every Wednesday afternoon, Najla posed for students at the Academy of Fine Arts. Going to see her at work might not seem appropriate for sorting out an emotional issue, but it was practical; Nader wouldn't be there. I would walk her to the nearby café to talk things over. I had to know if she'd just made a mistake and was ready to apologise, feeling as crushed and lovelorn as I was. Maybe the applause for his Hamlet had made Nader so euphoric that he'd just barged in to blurt out his gratitude for Najla's set design and she'd weakened momentarily, maybe even afraid a rejection would snap his fragile mind? No, they'd probably been at it for a while, Najla was reverting to her original self. She'd had enough of me and wanted to move on. Whatever, I had to hear it from her or I'd never cure this burning behind my eyes.

An apprehensive energy rolled me down to the School of Fine Arts. A colonial building that had once housed the Ministry of Justice, its walls of dark sandstone and long ornamented windows gave it an aura of authority. It was here, in its circular courtyard, that executions by hanging used to take place. But those ghosts had been dispelled by colourful new occupants: painters, drama students and musicians.

I positioned myself by the door to the room, whose window was veiled with a badly-hung curtain.

She was sitting on a wooden stool, her red curls tucked under a wig of long black hair that coiled round her neck and hung to the middle of her naked back. Her face was turned away. Only a slight angle of her breast was exposed to the busy pencils of at least twenty students. Thousands of inaudible strokes whipped her backside. My eyes were reading and interpreting the lines they were striving to copy, the details of a form whose content was unknown to them. Strangers who had never been in touch with the soul inside those ribs, never known with blind touch every pore and every vertebra beneath that skin, never smelled the scent of her sweat, never tasted the tang of her breast and the relish of her mouth. They might as well be sketching a vase, a tree, or an unstrung cello. The real benefactor of the experience was Najla herself. She was Van Gogh. They were mere potato eaters.

The rattle of an electric bell jolted me out of my thoughts. The sketchers quickly made their final touches, then began shuffling around like a flock of bats. I cursed those who lifted their easels and obstructed my view. I feared she would slip through an inner room to change and I'd lose her, but no, she was still there, getting up now. I expected her to peel off her wig, but she didn't. Then she leaned over at an angle to pick up her shawl . . . and I saw her breasts sag.

She wasn't Najla.

I ran off and hailed a taxi to Raouché. I begged the driver to step on it, please, a matter of urgency.

'What's the rush?'

'A problem at home.'

'Children?'

I shook my head.

'Must be a woman.'

I nodded. He nodded sagely and stopped talking.

Beirut's traffic added further to my despair, the bulky buses locked in their eternal warfare with the service taxis and the commuters crawling home from work. My driver was an old southerner of the If-you-are-in-a-hurry-drive-slowly school, though he did take a couple of shortcuts unknown to me. Poor, dingy alleys where kids seemed to be raining from balconies and men were permanently carved into corners smoking their water pipes.

Najla's apartment was eclipsing in the sunset. The shutters were closed, the little dots of light among the flower pots extinguished. The whole floor was shrouded in a darkness that fell down on me like a curse.

She's moved out, the Egyptian concierge said, maybe abroad. She doesn't live here any more. He shook his head: No, no letters, no messages, no address, nothing. Yes, yes, she emptied the apartment. No, nothing at all. No paintings.

I asked him for a key and put ten liras on the counter. He lifted his shoulders and pursed his lips, handing me the key.

The electricity wasn't connected, but lights from the surrounding buildings painted their silhouettes on the empty walls. The place had been stripped, made ready to rent out or sell. What hit me most was the lack of smell. The medley of paint, ripening fruit and incense was gone, leaving a gloomy vacuum in its wake.

I went out to the terrace. The southwesterly was gusting in tepid billows. Foamy waves were lashing the edge of Raouché's notorious lovers' leap like salivating wolves. You want me? You want Koko to jump and feed you tonight? Come and get me!

My broken heart has long since healed, but there are still days when I wish I'd kicked open that bathroom door, wish I'd broken Nader's neck.

Beirut
13 April 1977
Afternoon

8

As I dipped down into the Bekaa, the prospect of meeting its outlaws and attending a wedding in their fiefdom grew in appeal. I wondered what their lives were like now that the whole of Lebanon was outlaw. Normally their world was set apart from ours. They still lived by tribal traditions and codes of honour unknown to the rest of the world. And they dealt with normal society as if it was a leper. I imagined them rising above the pettiness of street thugs and war mongers. But why would they be welcoming the press on this of all days?

My fascination with outlaws went back to the Armenian desperadoes of my childhood. Especially Garo, who'd become legendary for his magical escapades and heroic confrontations with the police. A folk hero, whose outsiderdom was at the core of his tragedy.

Garo's family had fled Alexandretta in 1916, first to Aleppo and then to the banks of the Beirut River. There was no respite in the struggle to survive; the Ottomans tracked escapees all the way to Aleppo and beyond. Some were buried alive, others shot on sight and left in the open fields. Whole families perished like that. Garo's parents started out with nine children. Six of them survived. I grew up picturing Garo uprooted at the tender age of four – the same age I lost my parents – imagining his state of mind during the muffled panic of drifting through long cold nights on rugged roads, his hunger and the sudden neglect of his basic needs. I guess I wanted to give Garo a motive for rebelling against the world. Certainly fate was never merciful towards him. A few years after his family finally settled in Lebanon, his eldest brother, Antranic, was diagnosed with brain cancer. He was only eighteen. He suffered and died a terrible death. Garo was twelve. His brother's agony and subsequent death hit him so hard that he took a knife, made a deep cut in the crook of his arm and sat in a dark corner washing his blood with tears – 'Waiting to die,' as he said when he was found. From then on, death became an enemy Garo vowed to beat. The harshness of everyday life in the poor ghetto was his training camp. School was no haven for him; he was troubled and ready to burst at the slightest hostility. Punishing him physically was the only way his mother knew how to parent a child. It hardened him to a numbness that later became his most striking trait.

Every boy in Bourj Hammoud and the surrounding Armenian slums aspired to become Garo. Poor Armenian kids played at 'Garo and the Gendarmerie', changing the tragic end to Garo's credit. We emulated him in smaller ways, too. Break the rules, cross the line, dare the devils that come your way. Take and run. Steal cigarettes from shops and homes. Fool a street vendor. Grab clothes from washing lines. Gather junk from other people's yards and sell it to scrap metal dealers. It's what the streets of my childhood practised and preached. It never caused me sleepless nights. On the contrary, the adrenalin rushes during those 'operations' were terrific.

Occasionally I consulted Uncle Varouj: 'Say you're passing by and the police are chasing a criminal who drops a bag full of money. No one sees it but you. Would you tuck it under your arm and walk away or hand it over to the cops?'

'Take it,' Uncle Varouj said. Then he added, 'But be ready to lay low for a long time. And don't get too cocky.'

'What if I was caught?'

'It's not a crime to find money.'

'Dirty money?'

'You didn't soil it. You just picked it up.'

I was sure Aunty Clauda would disagree, so I never asked her.

And I never let my uncle know about my free-wheeling on the streets. Sorting out matters of principle with him was enough.

The year after I dropped out of school, I committed my first real felony. Getting away with it unscathed still gives me a thrill. Feeling somewhat righteous, I blackmailed a pederast barber who was touching up and bending many of the street boys. He'd close the main door and take his victim to the backyard. I loathed him, but I also saw in him potential for profit. One day I waited for him behind the yard's wall with a camera. I waited until I managed to click him in the act. Back in the shop, I developed the pictures and printed a few copies. I hid the prints and the film inside my sofa-bed and lay down, heart thudding, pondering my next move. Tens of scenarios went through my head. Should I send him a letter with a copy of the shots and ask him to meet me at the stadium after dark? Or should I go straight to him and face him nose to nose? Had I been the father of that boy I would no doubt have shot him. But I didn't want him dead. I wanted him to stop luring the boys and I wanted him to pay. I was good at calculation. How much money? And what was I going to do with it without being spotted? I couldn't go on shopping sprees. Uncle Varouj might not notice but Aunty Clauda would. Saving was for wimps. Money should be used to buy power. And power takes time. So don't go asking for a lump sum, bleed him on a weekly basis, and don't even think of letting anyone know. No one.

I tucked the pictures under my shirt and went down to the barber shop. The fear that burned my steps was also the heat that drove me. I went in, sat down, picked up a magazine from the coffee table and waited. When the barber finished his client I led him by the arm to his backyard. A tepid breeze was caressing the jasmine that climbed the wall. I remember the smell of jasmine, the honking of service taxis, the street vendors' cries. But mostly the barber's face when he took the blow. His knees buckled. He squatted and groaned, hugging his head in his arms. He nodded and nodded, biting the hook.

I wanted that money. I was building myself up in a merciless environment; ten liras a week was going to buy me the best gang on the street.

The deal lasted two years. Then the barber was caught and sent to jail. I'm no expert, but I guess there's a big difference between having crime as a career, and committing it opportunistically when it pops up in your path, especially if it's bloodless; between waking up every morning to a day of crime, and finding and keeping a bag of money.

9

The vast flat plain of the Bekaa, guarded by forbidding chains of mountains and domed with a pale erasable sky, was whetting my appetite for speed. I forgot whether I was heading to Dyarna or the Empty Quarter. To drive on and on after ages in a city where you can never get to fourth gear before hitting the next checkpoint was an amazing joy.

This fertile valley, once known as the warehouse of Rome, was Lebanon's breathing lifeline. Without it the land might cave in under the mass of its overwhelming mountains. It became a part of independent Lebanon after the Second World War, when the French and the British carved a new map for Greater Syria. The Maronite Patriarch, Hwayek, fought tooth and nail to include the Bekaa in Lebanon's map. But while most of Lebanon became a melting pot of confessions and semi-tribal families, part of the Bekaa remained wedded to its nomadic way of life. On the eastern side and further north there lived a dozen tribes.

During Ottoman times, Turkish merchants introduced the cultivation of hemp to the valley. A relatively easy crop to grow, hemp suited the laid-back life of those tribes. Then, when Lebanese Gold became famous during the drug-soaked sixties, real gold began to glitter in their hands. They sent their children to the best schools and universities. They built mansions to replace their shacks. And they flashed their new money for all to see: cars, clothes, furniture, all the latest electronic devices. Where there's money, there's politics. High officials became partners in the new trade, covering shipments and protecting drug lords, even permitting a tarmac road in the heart of the Bekaa to facilitate hash shipments. Immune from control, the cannabis birds carried Lebanon's most famous crop to the whole world. The World Health Organisation tried and failed to substitute sugar beet for hash in the valley, but it was too late. The demand for *seed* was huge, the gains irresistible.

Come the civil war, a new guest arrived in the hemp paradise: poppies. Experts from Iran and Turkey came to Baalbek with the gear and the know-how and started extracting heroin for the international market. Now Brown Sugar Lebo was added to the national produce.

Poppy and hemp pollen was filling the air, making me sing with joy. Thank you, Fathy, for this unexpected feeling of elation and –

Shit. I'd passed the seven Cyprus trees and the dirt track of my destination. I slowed down, did a U turn and started up the designated track. Boulders, ditches, deep winding cracks – my VW swayed and sneezed, the squeaking of the chassis was sounding a death rattle. They must have used hands for shovels to carve this road, leaving rocks protruding wherever they failed to extract them. Or maybe they left them on purpose in order to delay raids. Squinting against the glare and dust, I searched for Nader. The further I drove with no sign of him, the more I feared the worst. What if he's lost – I wasn't, I knew I wasn't. But him? He could be anywhere, doing anything. I didn't fancy arriving at an unknown village without my scribe. Nader, bloody Nader –

Yes! There he was, in the misty glare of the sun, trudging along ahead of me, a denim jacket slung over one shoulder, his hair sprinkled with the yellow dust of the road. And no car in sight.

'Where's your car?'

No answer. Not even a nod to acknowledge my presence. He just kept walking.

'Hop in, man. Come on.' I drove close but not too close. 'Get into the car, Nader!' I flung the door open for him.

He ducked as if being shot at and ran to the shade of a small, parched oak. There he sat on a rock and took out his pouch and his rolling papers. I decided to give the car a rest now that I'd found him, so I switched off the engine and leaned back, watching him roll his joint. He liked to use three glueless Damascus papers to form a rocket of considerable power. That extra thin rolling paper was his favourite. He bit the edges, passed them across the tip of his tongue and pressed them together to dry between his forearm and his thigh. Then he sprinkled a skimpy layer of tobacco on the weed and handled the rolling with such concentration you'd think he was preparing a real missile. He knew it was killing him. And kept going.

When he finished smoking he sleepwalked his thin body into the passenger seat. I glared at him as we bumped and swayed up the track. His mouth was pale blue, and his dry-glazed eyes were ogling the emptiness as if expecting an apparition. He must have been tripping hard. Unless he was playing one of his games with me just to avoid confrontation. Suddenly he stirred and pointed at the peaks of the mountain range ahead, like Columbus seeing America: 'There they are! The Samurai! They've landed! We're saved!'

'I should do you, Nader. I should push you into a deep valley for the hyenas to eat, and no one will ever know what happened to you. But I need to finish this job first. Are you with me?' Fuck him, if he didn't come round soon I'd click a few shots, scribble some notes for Fathy and leave him out here to rot.

Nader was still staring at a virtual horizon when the road ended abruptly in a rocky cul-de-sac. I stepped out and opened the passenger door for him. 'Yalla!'

He obliged without a word, stood up and looked around as if he'd been dropped from a space ship. Then he started up the footpath that snaked into the eastern foothills. With visible difficulty he put on his jacket against the cool breeze.

I followed him through low thistle, broom, wild thyme and gorse. I could smell, but not see, sticky fleabane, which seemed out of place in such dry scrub. Its strong balm scent took me back to the times when I came home with cuts and scratches and Aunty Clauda used fleabane paste to stop the bleeding. Up ahead were a few scattered stone cottages shaded by fig trees and vine pergolas. I could feel invisible eyes watching us. I could almost hear their mocking whispers: what the hell are those monkeys doing here?

Nader was mumbling something. I drew closer to him.

> He tries to melt the steel of hell's gate
> With his eyes
> But the gate remains frozen
> And now he's blind.

'Listen, you bugger. We have a job here. You know more about it than I do, but I'll do it with or without you. Do you read me?' I grabbed his arm, striving to connect with him.

He jerked away from me and began reciting from Hamlet: 'I loved her: forty thousand brothers could not, with all their quantity of love, make up my sum. What wilt thou do for her?'

'Love? You telling me that you are capable of love? Hah! Nader, this is Koko here. Don't I know you inside out? You've never loved anybody or anything. I don't think you loved your poor mother who laid her life like a rosary around you, or your wife or your son or Najla. You are incapable of love, because you are inhabited by your ghosts and demons twenty-four hours a day. You are one crazy bastard, Kunem Kezi.'

I turned away in disgust from his unblinking eyes and walked on. Then I heard him speak, quietly, normally. I looked back. 'Koko, read this.' He was tendering a cutting from a foreign newspaper, trying to focus his gaze towards me. It was a small-lettered item, most probably from the bottom of a gossip column of some tabloid:

88

Lebanese Outlaws Offer to Help End Civil War

The men, who could have chosen to become warlords, have instead opted out from the conflict. None of them consider themselves criminals. Rather, they are 'honour killers' who have simply executed the will of their tribes in the vendettas that have been going on for centuries in this part of Lebanon. 'We are as much victims of tradition as those we killed,' said Jaafar (not his real name). They have mixed feelings about the effect of the civil war on them. 'On the one hand, we are safer from police and army raids. On the other, we are being forgotten, our status is being eroded.' They claim they have a plan to stop the escalation of violence sweeping across Lebanon. All they are asking in return is amnesty and integration into a new society.

'I thought we were covering a tribal wedding. What's this?'
'Two birds with one stone.'
'This is a hot fart to seek attention, Nader. Where's your brain?'
'Look!'
For a split second I thought he was hallucinating again. But no, this time it was for real. A youth was coming towards us, his lean face tanned copper by the mountain sun, his hair greased back like Elvis, wearing tight Levis and a red polo shirt. He walked with a laid back gait like a mountain cowboy firmly rooted in his turf. Click, click. I was so fast I left him no time to pose or oppose.

'This is Hikmat,' Nader said, spreading his arm between the two of us.

'*Ya hala,*' Hikmat welcomed.

I was no stranger to the sub-text of language in this part of Lebanon; the nuances always meant more than the words. Hikmat's warmth inspired a sense of generosity, like someone handing you an open umbrella on a rainy day.

'This is Koko, the man himself,' Nader announced grandly.

We shook hands. 'You the one who shot the Israeli ass, huh?'
Hikmat grinned.

I was surprised that he remembered that shot from before the
war. I'd clicked it in the south, hanging out from the open door
of a speeding truck: an Israeli sentinel taking a dump, half his
buttocks smiling at us across the border. Fathy had this caption
for it: 'The Wall of Good Will, Open Sesame!' The next day it
was all over the country. People were doubled up with laughter.
I went to Fathy's desk expecting congratulations. Empty. I went
to the men's; when he's not behind his desk (bushy eyebrows, a
sly smile permeating his face as he whips a manuscript into
shape with his red biro) Fathy is in the men's. Not that day, but
Emile was: 'Spin upstairs, on the double – Fathy's already there.'

I knew from old-timers that the boss had never called Fathy
to his office before; he would just phone or drop by casually
to discuss a hiccup, and there hadn't been many of those to
speak of.

'The whole country's laughing,' Emile concluded, shaking his
pants.

'I know – time for a raise!'

'Fat chance!'

Ustaz Burhan's office. The man himself looking thunderous.
And Fathy, arms folded, head tilted, eyes shut, catching the flak
with nirvanic serenity. The boss was addressing him all the
while I was standing by the door waiting in vain for at least
a gesture to sit. He was stressing some 'strategic differences'
between freedom of expression and professional responsibility:
'The southerners have been losing lives and property for decades,
they'll see an insult in that shot, an Israeli ass in their faces.
We're not a tabloid; we're the leading newspaper in this country
and the most admired in the Arab world. Why? Because we
care. We weigh things carefully. We understand the deepest
sensitivities. We are emphatic. We are cultured, sophisticated.
We coin new expressions that instantly become common usage

throughout the Arab press. And we are the most quoted news source in the Middle East. Let us pray that no international newspaper reproduces this terrible shot.'

I wasn't fired that day or even given a dressing-down, just waved away with a curt gesture; the gesture of one who refrains from saying something hard for fear of hurting you.

Hikmat would have been only a child when that shot was printed. Clearly there was more to him than at first appeared. He was better informed than one might imagine; as we continued treading uphill, he expressed his sorrow about Manal. They'd heard the news on the radio. 'His only child,' he said, sounding much older than his years. 'The apple of his eye. May God give him strength.'

Soon the sticky fleabane revealed its sunny green leaves edging a stream rolling down from the peak of the arid mountain. Its aroma and the silvery trickle of fresh water drew me to the stream like a thirsty horse. I kneeled down, put my camera inside the fleabane shrub and drank deeply. Then I plunged my whole head into the stream. Fuck the Pasha, this is good! Nader followed suit, but more ceremoniously, as if performing ablutions at a holy shrine; he bent down, raised his arms to the sky, then bowed and gathered the water piously in his palms. But the ceremony was over as soon his face touched the water. The freezing shock to his body must have shaken something loose in him. When we resumed walking, he was zigzagging like a drunk through the twisted detours around the rocks. Hikmat fell back to stroll with me.

'I could drink from that all day. Where is it coming from?' I asked.

'From Yammouneh, on top of the mountain.'

Squinting, I could now see, far beyond the village ahead, the source of the stream. A short distance below it were a couple of stone cottages, tiny and tucked into the curve of the land like warts in an armpit. A short washing line hung between them and on it a white garment flailed the air.

Hikmat read my puzzlement. 'A witch lives up there,' he said matter-of-factly. 'She roams the mountain all alone, but she's harmless.'

'And next door?'

'It's for her donkey. The whitest donkey you've ever seen.'

The contrast between the fast drumming tempo of Beirut and the vast, silent proximity of the sky was disarming. We were reaching an altitude some eighteen hundred metres above sea level. Every breath was like a sweep of disinfectant. I was shedding my gloom by the minute. 'This is a stunning place. Have you been here long?'

'It's too barren for me. I prefer the woods on the other side of the mountain. But we can't complain. My father says this place has been a refuge for people like us since the Ottoman rule.'

'Did you tell Nader that?'

Hikmat chuckled. 'That man knows everything. He arrived yesterday. He talked to everyone. Then he performed a play for us. There was a full moon last night.'

'Hamlet, was it?'

Hikmat nodded uncertainly. I guessed Nader had provided no introduction to the 'play', just thrown it all out to a bunch of people who'd never heard of the English bard, let alone his tormented hero. Typical. 'Experimenting with a raw audience', he calls it. He'd done it before in many ways. 'If I am good I ought to make the birds catch their breath mid-air. Otherwise I am shit,' he once told me. Birds never paid much attention to his antics, but people did stop in their tracks to watch, whether he was performing a play or standing on his head in the middle of Hamra Street, freaking out the passing cars, a sign wrapped round his chest: Stop Honking! Tens of such incidents illustrate his 'street performances.' I only witnessed a few, but at the Horse Shoe there are even historians who've recorded his silly pranks, dates and times and all.

Hikmat seemed eager to talk more but uncertain how to continue, so I offered a sure-fire winner: 'How's trade these days?'

'Great!' he beamed. 'We're making oil out of second and third rate resin. The gringos like it because it's potent and light to carry. One kilo of oil is worth ten of pressed resin.' Hikmat's vitality was engaging.

'But are you selling? No airport, hardly any communications, I can't imagine who's buying, or how.'

'We're selling,' Hikmat boasted. 'The highest ranks from all the militias come here together. Enemies on the front line, partners in seed, you could say. '

'Local consumption only?'

'The sea is open, Koko. Your story will advertise us abroad, big time.'

We talked as we walked. Hikmat was a cheeky lad with a liking for the wheeler-dealer world. In normal circumstances he would make a good politician. But his mind was set on the hash trade despite the dangers. School was boring compared to making contacts and deals and sales strategies. If his father agreed on planting and processing opium they would become millionaires in no time. 'But he's stubborn, you know,' he said, knocking on his forehead. He'd picked up enough English and French to get by, even some German, and was going to learn more English from his American girlfriend, the one he was 'planning to have very soon.' This would be a Jessica Lange look-alike. He'd seen her in a pirated copy of the recent King Kong remake – he'd watched it twelve times in Baalbek – and he 'knew' she was coming. 'One day she'll be walking up that road, and we'll hit it off at first sight. I swear to God, this is going to happen.'

'Would you marry an American?'

'Why not? It only takes a few words to make her a Muslim, no problem, and then she'll take me to Hollywood!'

10

We had reached a small stone cottage. It must have been locally quarried. The largest stones forming its base became gradually smaller as the walls rose. An ancient fig tree spread its branches over much of the western corner. On the northern side, nearest the stream, we climbed up three cement steps on to a small terrace – clearly last night's open-air theatre. On its far side, opposite the steps, was a straw mat with cushions, some leaning against the cottage's front wall. Between the steps and the seating was an open door, from which a female voice sang out: *'Ya hala!'*

'My stepmother, Abla,' murmured Hikmat.

A moment later, she appeared on the threshold, smiling, palm on chest, bowing slightly.

'There's rosemary, that's for remembrance: pray you, love, remember,' Nader quoted Hamlet again, and bowed back. But this Ophelia didn't seem to pay him much attention.

I was smitten. I'd seen fair-haired and fair-skinned people in this part of the valley before – some say they're the descendants of the Crusaders – but usually they were baked by the sun into a craquelure effect. Not Abla. She was pure platinum, with azure eyes and a haunting grace. Black leggings covered her ankles beneath her long flowery dress. Her hair was wrapped casually in an embroidered scarf. She gestured us to take a seat on the mat and came down the steps to a stone hearth by the stream, her wooden clogs clapping like an encore. She lit the fire and ambled back inside. Her every movement was delivering a clear telepathic message: I know that you're wondering about me. And that you'll fail to resist asking. Take your time.

I longed to click her and promised myself to steal her into my lens by hook or by crook. Considering the strict codes of conduct around Muslim females, my imagination was trespassing on forbidden grounds. But it had been ages since I'd felt this gutsy urge to click something with real pleasure. Who but a sadist could enjoy shooting the aftermath of car bombs, sniper victims, burned houses, dragged bodies, mutilations? After the Ein al-Rumaneh bus carnage, a duel of massacres had begun between the Palestinians and their allies versus the Christian alliance. Clicking them all, it became difficult to tell them apart. As well as those gory scenes, I followed furtive politicians darting between hideaways and clicked endless Arab summits, as regular as recesses in a pathetic game of soccer.

Before he was kidnapped, our boss joined a Comity for Peace and Dialogue. He was desperate to make a difference after everything he'd written had been drowned by deafening explosions. He knew it was a professional sin, knew too that it wouldn't change a thing, and yet he went for it, until the snowball of violence swept away the Comity and with it the boss's patience. He cursed everybody who was making Lebanon a scapegoat: Israel for having a ball while the Palestinians were killed, dislocated, or deported; Syria for playing saviour while in reality recapturing territory peeled from it by the Sykes-Picot treaty; Egypt for preparing a unilateral peace agreement with Israel which would make Lebanon as vulnerable as a lamb in a slaughter house. While he and other scribes were raging on paper, the click people were becoming anaesthetised by the tragedy. No wonder my lens longed to caress Abla.

The cushions set out on the terrace confirmed that she had been expecting us. Nader straightaway made himself at home. He lotused on the mat and sucked the air down into his abdomen, keeping it there for a moment before letting it out slowly. He was, as always, within his aura. His eyes resembled those of a hibernating lizard. His chest gurgled.

My senses were basking in the soothing therapy of pure air, and the silence was easing my troubled spirit. I didn't know what to expect. The part of me that was eager to get the job done ASAP, get back home to Nishan, put on a suit and hurry to pay my condolences to my boss was having a snooze with eyes wide open. Hikmat went inside and fetched a copper teapot. He put it on the young fire and then fed the flame with more twigs. They crackled, spitting little stars between his legs.

Coming back from the hearth, he whispered over my shoulder, 'Nader took a blue pill. Want one?'

'Who gave it to him?'

'Me. Last night after the play.'

'And after that?'

'He went to the valley.'

Shit. If Nader had taken LSD last night, he must be out of the big high and using joints to level the inevitable crash. I imagined his brain a poked hive of wasps seething with a deafening drone. What kind of article would he write in this state? And where was his car? If he'd left it in a ditch he'd never remember where. The magic carpet of this tranquil place began fraying. I asked Hikmat about the car.

'No worries. We took it to smuggle someone out of the Bekaa.' He made it sound like an everyday chore.

'When will it be back?'

'Someone will bring it. Don't busy yourself with it. The car's safe. My grandmother is driving it and – '

'Your – '

'Oh yeah, and she'll defend it with a Colt 45. You don't want to meet her on a dark night,' he added proudly.

Hikmat was unruffled by my astonishment. He explained, 'My uncle disobeyed her. He married someone from our rival tribe, so she shot him in the buttock. Before he gets out of hospital, she has to lay low for a while. She shouldn't have shot him there, you know.'

A bleeding groom's backside and a gun-toting granny fleeing with Nader's car. Great. If the car fails to show up I'll be stuck with Nader, unless he stays behind; and if he does, our story will be at risk.

At the clinking of tea glasses and the clatter of wooden clogs, Nader opened his eyes, ready to be served. Hikmat held the tray as his stepmother poured the tea. She bowed graciously and handed us the glass cups, her forehead tightening over the Arabian sabres of her eyebrows. I liked her as much for her dignified bearing as for her striking beauty. She was so close, I had to resist touching her hand.

The sound of the rippling stream kept us company while we sipped the extra-sweet black tea. It sang of life in this otherwise barren wilderness.

We were nearly finished when heavy crunching footsteps on stones cut through the liquid music. A man was approaching the terrace, a lamb tucked under his arm. He was in his traditional sleeveless Sittac-Rosa and a rough grey sherwal wrapped at the waist with a thick leather belt. Sharp green eyes and a thin brown moustache completed the biblical portrait. Rashly, I snapped his picture without permission.

Hikmat gave a reassuring laugh and stood up to introduce us. We shook hands. His name was Yousef, a shepherd from nearby Deir al-Ahmar grazing his flock in the valley. Hikmat's father had asked him to bring a lamb for the wedding. He pointed out that his sad-eyed animal was a milk lamb, just been weaned. He spoke firmly, in anticipation of the customary haggle.

'How much?' Hikmat asked.

'Ten liras,' said Yousef.

Hikmat responded with a dismissive smile and started checking out the lamb as if it were a flawed second-hand garment.

Yousef got the message. He stirred a little, then changed

tactics, his voice softening. 'I drove the flock all the way here hoping that Our Lady of Bishwat would make me reach you in time. She did, bless her sacred feet.'

Yousef's evocation of the miraculous Madonna, treasured as much by Bekaa Shiites as by Christians, was a clever commercial move, tapping into a soft spot to make his adversary put heart over wallet.

Hikmat's shoulders slumped, recognising the blow. Then he smiled again, pursing his lips. His eyes had a foxy glint. 'So, how's your old man doing these days? And your dear mother? I hope they are both well?'

'Alhamdulillah,' said Yousef, acknowledging with a brave face that Our Lady's mediation was out the window. 'They both ask after you. They consider you a son.'

'If that's so, why don't you step up and join us for a sip of tea. Standing there like a stranger doesn't make us brothers, does it?'

'God bless your threshold, brother Hikmat. We have a legacy of breaking bread together. But I left the flock with the dogs. You know how it is.'

'You still have that German Shepherd with the cut-off ears? A bloody wolf, that dog.'

'That dog is no more. I have two kelpies. They are too nervous when left alone.'

A subtle cock fight was growing between the two. It wasn't all about money. A lot of pride was involved. Traditionally the merchant aims high, the buyer goes below reason, and the small talk in between is a show of wit between duelling minds. It went back to when people swapped goods for goods, when essential components of the bartering were credibility, reputation, and honour. It is of course a priority to make a sale, but it also matters to whom and with what level of mutual satisfaction.

'Put the animal down and come over here. I want you to know our guests properly; they are yours too.' Hikmat's tone had mellowed.

Yousef hesitated. This was a parry he didn't expect. 'Have we agreed on the price?' He kept his ground.

'Pray there will never be disagreement between us, brother Yousef,' Hikmat said languidly.

'Inshallah,' the shepherd murmured without conviction. Hikmat's feigned nonchalance didn't fool him one bit. He was, after all, the only available meat provider. There were guests involved and the celebration must be getting closer by the minute, so the rope wasn't pulling towards Hikmat as much as he liked to believe. Still, the client is king until the sale is done. And I guessed both men knew their limits; Hikmat wouldn't go as far as humiliating Yousef, knowing that the latter in turn wouldn't put the sale at risk.

A puff from Nader's joint brushed the thin nostrils of Yousef's nose. He twitched a muscle or two but his focus stayed on the sale. Abla stood at the door watching with detached interest. She probably foresaw the final outcome and was patiently waiting for the conclusion, like the ending of a movie she'd seen a thousand times.

The lamb's ears were twitching their own message: I hope you fail to agree.

The subtle tension between the two young men was broken when an older man came walking up the track. He was striding towards us with a proud upright posture, clad in a black keffiah, black shirt and black sherwal, radiating authority. Abla lifted her hand in a hasty salute and went indoors. Hikmat sprang to attention: 'My father,' he announced, 'Am Hussein.'

'Hala!' Am Hussein gave the shepherd a friendly but assertive push towards the centre of the terrace. There was an ancient warning in the man's eyes. His forbidding mien halted me from clicking him. We shook hands. His grip was rock hard, yet reassuring. 'You've come up here to celebrate with us and to listen to us. Thank you for taking the trouble.' He smiled like a diplomat. 'We regard you people of the pen as fellow-fugitives. Welcome.' He turned first to Yousef and then to Hikmat: 'What's the gap between you two?'

'Five liras,' both hagglers said in unison.

'Five liras it is.' He took the lamb, placed it between his legs and leant over to feel its ribs. 'It's a milk lamb all right, but its mother has been as stingy with her feed as you are greedy with its price.' The joke dispelled the rest of the tension. Am Hussein elbowed Yousef's shoulder playfully. 'No more haggles, just give our guests a little entertainment, they've come a long way.' He reached into his pocket and produced the conciliatory note.

Yousef took it. Then he grimaced as if freezing a sneeze or trying hard to remember something. For a second I thought he was in pain, a toothache perhaps. Then, out of nowhere, came the sound of a double-reed flute, the traditional minjayra, inseparable companion of shepherds, filling the air with a thin hum. But where was the flute? Yousef's hands remained at his sides. He hadn't moved one inch. I came closer, and closer, scrutinising his distorted face. It wasn't until I was almost at kissing distance that I noticed the faint vibration of his lips. I looked at Am Hussein and Hikmat. They were smirking like teenagers watching a prank.

'Good on you, brother Yousef,' said Am Hussein. Everybody cheered.

Yousef took his other five liras from Hikmat and poured himself a glass of tea. So far, he had avoided eye contact with Nader and me. Perhaps he judged we were hash buyers better ignored, or just preferred to keep his nose out of other people's business. But now he was under investigation. Nader wanted to know how he could produce not only the perfect sound of the shepherds' flute, but also the melody.

Yousef recited his story with the naivety of a child in a session of show and tell: 'One day I got lost far into the mountains. I was scared. I was twelve years old and all alone in the deep silence with a flock and no minjayra.' He paused to see if we'd registered the seriousness of his situation. 'So I prayed and prayed and prayed, pleading with the Madonna to help me, until, somehow I found a minjayra in my throat. It was a miracle.'

'A miracle indeed,' said Am Hussein solemnly. It was strangely moving to see such a thick-skinned outlaw still believing in miracles.

I'm not religious, but I do believe that faith is miraculous. I've seen first-hand enough evidence of faith's works to convince me that either there's a higher power hovering over us and responding to our pleas, or that man is a living deity capable of performing miracles through faith. More often than not the miracles I encountered were of the meek, the downtrodden and the simple-hearted. I've clicked and listened to people healed of fatal diseases and lifelong deformities filling the sky with praise, just because they believed that God, or one of His many messengers, had cured them.

Once I walked into a poor man's home where a miracle had been announced. I verified beyond a shadow of doubt that he'd been crippled for twenty-seven years due to an accident at work. Finally his prayers had been answered. I saw him walking normally. The pictures, the lifelong neighbours, the medical reports, the lack of any financial motive – all this, yes, but mostly the state of utter surprise from the man himself; a surprise no one could fake, let alone a simple builder. It was uncanny and left me stunned for hours.

In my own upbringing there was no denial of God, but neither did we pray at home. Aunty Clauda had a peculiar relationship with Him: she argued with Him. Her main gripe was that He wouldn't let us understand Him. 'Why must You be so secretive, so ambiguous? Why must You allow the atrocities of this world and do nothing to stop them? Put Your cards on the table, stop hiding behind religion,' she would grumble. 'I know You're there! I don't need preachers to teach me that!' she'd continue, baptising the street with a bucket of dirty water.

Though Uncle Varouj lent his wife's philosophy a humouring ear, he stopped short of voicing his own opinion. His business with Him was nobody's business. But, socially, they rarely missed Sunday Mass. It was a valued occasion for meeting and greeting others, and a tradition that went back to the first years of Diaspora, when churches constituted the cornerstone for reconstructing Armenia in Lebanon.

Suddenly we heard the shuffle of sheep. Two mongrels were leapfrogging over them until the whole flock was lined up along the stream. 'They heard me,' said Yousef, smiling. 'They hear me from the other side of the valley,' he added proudly. Now that his flock was at hand, Yousef relaxed. He even accepted a refill of tea.

The little lamb wobbled down to join its kin unhindered – there seemed to be a silent consensus to allow it a short goodbye. It pushed its way to the stream and disappeared, shrouded by its elders.

Yousef let it drink its fill, then retrieved it from the flock, gave it back to Hikmat, wished us a joyous wedding ceremony and strolled down before his flock, playing his minjayra, biblical still.

Abla brought a large copper platter and set it in the centre of the straw mat: thin mountain bread, bunches of green oregano, watercress, thyme, spring onions, mint, and a bowl of shining black olives. While our main course was left alone to graze by the stream, we nibbled, sipping sweeter-than-sweet tea. Am Hussein anointed the Persian tobacco of his water pipe with a hint of hash, remarking that 'only alcohol is haram in Islam.' Then he added, 'Unless our Prophet didn't know about this wicked plant.'

After a few leisurely puffs, he cleared his throat and put down the hose: 'We are honoured by your visit. We appreciate your crossing so many treacherous obstacles in order to reach our humble abode. You are welcome to stay with us as long as you wish. Stay until this war is over if you like.'

He spoke with a calm wisdom that stemmed from an innate capacity to impose order on disorder. Hardly your standard outlaw. Or so it seemed to me. But it affected Nader as well. To my surprise, he began taking notes. Usually he didn't bother, just asked a lot of questions, absorbed every word, and produced a piece somewhere between magic realism and live radio reporting. Now, for once, he was looking like a normal reporter.

Am Hussein went on: 'To be born into a tribal way of life makes you an outsider to the wider society. It entraps you even when you manage to escape.' He looked at us, one at a time, making sure his prologue was endorsed.

I nodded. Nader held up his pen reassuringly.

'My brother was killed in a vendetta that's been going on for generations,' Am Hussein continued. 'He was a teacher working in Zahleh. They shot him on the school steps in front of his students. There was no personal reason for killing him; his only link to the family was his name. He was an outsider to the cycle of our tribal life and never agreed with its vendettas. We knew who did it. Two small-time thugs of zero value. Killing them was not going to avenge him, which made the situation even more difficult. I reminded the elders that my brother always advocated ending the blood calendar we lived by and that he would not rest in peace if his desire to stop the vendettas was ignored. Surprisingly, they did take his wish on board. They tried to mediate, asking our rivals to deliver the culprits to the law and move on towards a truce. But the request was turned down, leaving us no choice. I was chosen to do the job; of all the family members, I was the least conspicuous. I was a smuggler, living abroad much of the time. So you see, the rival tribe would never expect me to risk losing a comfortable life in Europe.'

Am Hussein was relating his story slowly, editing each section with a sip of tea or a draw at his water pipe. 'The chosen target was a doctor, a brilliant surgeon who'd just got back from France to take up a prominent position at the Hotel Dieu hospital. "Kill him during his comeback celebration. Let him fall into his father's lap. Let his death hurt more than your brother's. They threw away a rare chance of peace. Let them pay the price." That was the order. I couldn't refuse. Not because I agreed with it but because refusing meant severing all my connections. I would become a pariah. I was thirty-six years old and dependant on my tribe.'

He recounted, with restrained emotion, how he'd been driven in a truck loaded with sheep, sitting in the middle of the flock and waiting for a special horn signal from the driver indicating their arrival at the closest possible range to the party. 'We'd spotted a dirt road above the terrace where I could aim solely at my target from a comfortable distance. Unfortunately, nothing works out exactly as planned. Two other people were wounded in the attack.' Am Hussein's voice sank and he shifted his gaze from us. Those two collateral victims seemed to weigh on him more than slaying the young doctor. 'They were guests. They had nothing to do with it,' he said sadly.

After the drive-by shooting, the truck carried on to a barn some distance away. Am Hussein was unloaded with the flock. He remained in the barn for two nights until it was possible to sneak him out. 'I smelt so awful, the driver who rescued me wrapped his face in his keffiah all the way to Dyarna.'

He glanced at the open door of the cottage as if anticipating Abla's appearance, but she was busy deep inside the house. We could hear her clattering in the kitchen. He lowered his voice. 'The mission was not yet fulfilled. I was already married to Hikmat's mother. She lives in Amsterdam, taking care of the business. But I had to marry my brother's widow as well. This is how things are done around here,' he said. 'She stays in the family. Protected. Cared for.'

Nader shut his notebook. He seemed dazed, as if awakened from a disturbing dream. 'The chain of events,' he mused. He cupped his chin and leaned forward: 'You became a smuggler because the Bekaa has been producing nothing but hashish. You became an executioner because your tribe is your only axis of belonging. And you married a second time because it was the only way to shelter your sister-in-law. Nothing happens to you of your own free will.'

Am Hussein nodded. I'm not sure he fully endorsed Nader's conclusion. Was he nodding agreement? Or indifference? Or silently asking Are you analysing me or interviewing me? But in a society like this one is compelled to take things at face value. Bluntness is seen as lack of wisdom. From an early age tribesmen and women are taught to keep their thoughts to themselves and behave strategically with others. In tribal life the mind must be as much a fighter as the body.

Any further thoughts were curtailed when Nader began stirring and gasping for air. I figured his brain was howling for a fix. He gave Hikmat a pleading look. Hikmat got the message, went inside and came back with a plastic bag and a tin ashtray. He deposited them in front of Nader, who handed him some money. Am Hussein frowned and looked away, embarrassed at his son's flagrant dealing.

I was pissed off. I put down my camera, yanked Nader up by the arm and dragged him, bobbing like a flat tyre, behind the cottage. I rammed him against the wall. 'What is going on here, Nader? Are we here to get wasted or what?'

'Just this last one. I paid for it,' he pleaded. He was so shaken by my sudden aggression he began to tremble. I released him, but not before stabbing my nose into his forehead: 'Get the job done and go fuck yourself elsewhere. All right?'

When we returned, Am Hussein tapped the cushion beside him, inviting me to sit. The fact that I'd interrupted the conversation so abruptly didn't seem to faze him. Clearly he knew why and was now easing the tension the diversion had created. I sat down, cross-legged, my camera on my lap.

'Have you heard of Garo?' he asked.

It was like asking an Arab if he'd heard of Ali Baba.

He sensed my surprise. He leaned slightly towards me as if entrusting me with a special confidence. 'Garo stayed here for a while, you know. He was one of us. We shared bread and salt with him and we slept many a night with him in the open when we were sneaking him out to Syria. We also did business with his mother, Nevart. You must have been in your early teens when Garo was shot,' he smiled. 'Do you remember what happened?'

How could I forget? The haunting image of Garo's naked body riddled with bullets, spread across the front page of the *Daily Sun*, came back to me like a spasm from a dormant ulcer. I told Am Hussein what I remembered: police chief Kiwan swooping down on Baddawi with tanks and armoured vehicles. It was a proper offensive. Garo and a couple of his men held out for seven or eight hours. When Garo felt the siege tightening, he ordered his men to flee and fought alone, retreating into the maze of alleyways and shacks. He got hit in the left thigh. A butcher hid him in the boot of his car and sneaked him out to a mountain village where he sought refuge with an old couple, very simple Armenians of the old school. The butcher and one of Garo's men were arrested. It was only a matter of hours before the frustrated gendarmes would arrive and spray the hideout with bullets. But Garo wasn't going to give up. He jumped out of the window into a vine pergola and fought back until his last bullet, the one he fired into his own head.

When I stopped speaking, I thought I heard a sniffle. I looked up to see Abla just disappearing into the cottage again. Perhaps the story had reawakened a pain of her own. Hikmat looked as if he were staring bleakly at his own future.

But Am Hussein objected to the end of my tale. 'Garo was capable of taking his own life all right, but in the heat of battle, counting his bullets to save the last one for himself would have taken great concentration. Also, when his body was brought to the morgue, his head was unscathed.'

Like a child told the truth about Santa, I was crestfallen. For us Armenians, Garo was a hero. Only heroes could choose their exit, singing gloriously their last aria. Demystifying him with technical facts was hard to swallow. 'I beg your pardon, Am Hussein, you seem to remember all the details of Garo's demise. How?' I said, questioning the source rather than the content.

'It's like football,' he replied calmly. 'Wouldn't you remember and discuss over and over a striking moment of the game? Garo's last battle remained the talk of the underworld for years. We knew what kind of man brigadier Kiwan was. All he wanted was to get the job done. Showing off didn't interest him. He didn't even care about promotion. When he took his men to Garo's hideout he made sure to warn the old couple, through the village mayor, hence giving Garo a last chance to surrender. Garo wouldn't do that but he did opt to spare his protectors further trouble, so he jumped out of the window, not knowing he would hit a vine pergola. He was already injured, and now he was also trapped: isolated, surrounded, an easy target at the end of his tether. He just kept shooting until the last cartridge. No way could he have had the presence of mind to count his bullets.' Am Hussein wiped his face as if wiping away the last scene of Garo's life. 'When you experience close-range shoot-outs, only half of your brain functions, the crazy half. The other half is waiting to greet you at the doorway to hell.'

Am Hussein was all too convincing. I wanted to change the subject, to avoid any more dethroning of my childhood king. 'Have you been in many shoot-outs, Am Hussein?'

He gave me a long, deliberating look, then leaned over as if about to take off his shoes. Instead, he lifted the hem of his black sherwal, showing a right leg completely disfigured, its thin brown flesh sticking to the bone, the muscle fibres bunched. Am Hussein didn't look up, giving me enough time to register, but I sensed that a click here was not recommended. God only knows how he still managed to walk as well as he did. Then he covered his leg like smoothing a blanket over a sleeping child, and heaved a deep breath. Still avoiding eye contact, he began unbuttoning his black, collarless shirt with a surgeon's caution.

Hikmat stirred uneasily. He locked his arm into his father's and turned his eyes away. Apparently he didn't want us to see the bullet wounds on his father's chest. One of them was so deep I could see the heart pulsing inside.

Am Hussein disengaged his arm and looped it around his son's shoulder. 'It happened in Holland. We were delivering a shipment in Rotterdam. We'd cleared customs easily, loaded the truck with a ton of hash camouflaged in tinned hummus and reached our destination. It was raining heavily. Bad weather has always been friendly to smugglers. We were too relaxed to expect foul play and there was no reason to doubt our Dutch connection. But we didn't know that there'd been a change of plan. Instead of unloading it for pickup and distribution in the next night, our partners had contracted another party to finish the job that same night. Unfortunately their driver was tracked down by the police. We were inside, tasting the resin with a cup of tea, when the lights went out. We heard the police warning, but before we could make a move we heard gunshots. It was never clear who had started it. All hell broke loose in a matter of seconds. A storm of gunfire swept over the warehouse. The worst thing that has ever happened to me was handling a weapon I'd never used before in pitch darkness. It was half revolver, half automatic with an awkward magazine. My frustration was more painful than the injuries. But we fought back. We kept the police at bay long enough to escape through a series of back doors. One of our Dutch partners put me in the boot of his car and drove off like a bat from hell. I can still see my blood dripping on the black cobblestones. I was in that near-coffin for four hours, in a pool of blood. I stayed hidden in a country house for two months. All my wounds healed without proper medical attention. Those guys were amazing. Although we lost the shipment, they insisted on paying half the price and took care of me like a brother. The Dutch smugglers may not sound like much but they are a breed apart.'

Abla had quietly rejoined us during this narration. Now she brushed her husband's back softly with the palm of her hand. I sensed her touch was a subtle message: you are not your brother, but I love you just the same. Am Hussein was still holding his son close to him. At last I understood why he'd evoked Garo's story and then shown us his dreadful wounds. Like most teenagers Hikmat wasn't going to accept advice, but he might be deterred when shown the darker side of his dreams.

11

A man's voice was calling from afar. It hovered above us, rich in vowels, unbroken, like a sail in a steady wind. But distance diluted his words. Our hosts, however, seemed to understand. Hikmat looked expectantly at his father. Abla's face was a silent question mark. Am Hussein raised his palm as a stop sign and drew slowly on his water pipe. After a few seconds of pondering, he spoke. 'I was in two minds about this wedding,' he said. 'These days a happy event can easily turn into a tragedy. Many young men are now trigger-happy, shooting like they want to kill the sky. But with God's watch over our guests and the reassurances given to me . . .' He stroked his moustache, gazing on the empty sky. 'I still say, let us all go.' He stood up. We stood up. 'Get ready, my dear,' he said tenderly to Abla. She blushed and hurried inside.

I helped Hikmat tidy up and extinguish the remains of the fire with a splash of water from the stream. Am Hussein picked up the lamb and tucked it under one arm, no longer a smuggler but a shepherd with his lamb. Abla reappeared. She'd rolled back her headscarf, releasing a cascade of golden hair all the way to her waist. She'd added a flowery shawl to her shoulders and put on some low-heeled black shoes. They were only little touches but they transformed her into a bright-eyed young woman up for an outing. Endearingly, she put her thin hand in her husband's, like an eyelid closing peacefully.

Without further ado, we emulated mountain goats, jumping over the stream, one after another, and fell into single file heading north on a narrow path. Am Hussein and Abla took the lead. At their heels Nader was asking questions. I followed close behind him. Every now and then Hikmat, at the rear, dashed stones across the scrub. There was nothing there but grey rocks and dusty green shrubs looking evanescent in the glare of the sun. I clicked a couple of mating lizards on a bed of stone before Hikmat interrupted them with a near miss and they slipped away, as lovers caught unawares always do.

Am Hussein was answering Nader's relentless questions about every aspect of tribal weddings:

'In the old days, a young man courted a maiden at her home before daring to involve his folks. He would sit with the rest of her family around the open fire. Eventually the maiden would take a little stick and gather a small pile of ashes before her. If she pulled the pile towards her it meant yes, if she pushed it towards him the answer was no.' I savoured the mixture of tension and tenderness in this silent courting, so different from current practice. Am Hussein must have read my mind. He went on: 'Nowadays they can meet secretly or openly, depending on circumstances, but the final decision is not theirs. The families decide. Those who choose to elope pay a high price. They become pariahs, disowned. Sometimes their act may entail a bloody response. Marriages are meticulously arranged. They involve not only the couple and their respective families, but also a whole world of tradition and social relations.'

'In the bourgeois circles of Beirut, marriages are still arranged. How is it different out here?' Nader asked.

Am Hussein nodded and went on to describe the tribal process in detail, starting with the preliminaries: a group of people visiting the maiden's family to test the ground. They won't be too closely related to the suitor. In order to avoid embarrassment in case of a negative response, they'll hint indirectly at the possibility of the match. If the maiden's people show positive interest, then the prospective in-laws will be notified. They will formally ask for a meeting. This will be led by a venerable elder. Am Hussein deepened his voice, impersonating an august sheikh: 'Most dear sir, madam. We are here in the honourable quest of your daughter's hand. It is a great honour and a source of pride for us to become your in-laws. We wish to continue the long line of acquaintance between our families. We hope to receive a favourable answer. He is our son, and she is our daughter, and they are both equal in our hearts.'

'Your son is not worthy of our angel! Never darken our doorway again!' Nader scowled, imitating a rebuff from the bride's father. Am Hussein and Abla laughed.

'But when a promise is made between families it is hard for the young men and women to go against it,' Am Hussein continued. 'My father was sixteen years my mother's senior, he'd seen her in her crib. She'd clutched at his finger so strongly that he asked for her hand then and there. And despite his harsh nature, they had a happy marriage. Nowadays some couples break all the rules to be together and end up divorced.'

'How about money? Is that a factor? ' Nader asked.

'Not as much as you might imagine. It's better to give your daughter to an honest shepherd than to a millionaire of murky provenance.'

'A smuggler?'

'Not murky. But a thief or a politician is.'

Hikmat was still throwing stones, aiming now at salamanders and fidgety little birds. This place is his playground, I thought. He must know each nook and cranny in this scrub like the palm of his hand. He could probably walk it for miles blind-folded. And he wants to swap it for Hollywood and a Jessica Lange look-alike, not yet knowing how much he'll long for it after he's gone.

The dirt path stopped abruptly at the edge of a cliff. The wind hit us hard. Stalled in the flow of a gale, I stooped to escape the invisible power, then whirled back, again and again, the gusts turning me into a kite barely anchored by invisible strings. Around us, the ominous mountains groaned like pre-historic beasts stirring into action. Even the ground beneath our feet was shaking.

Far below us, at least a hundred metres down, was a green space as wide as a football field, shored up by the rocky hills. Several large colourful tents had been erected on both the near and the far sides of the field. Women carrying trays moved in and out of the tents. A waterfall tumbled from a wide mouth in the rocks, pouring into a ravine on the northern side of the green.

A tandem of mules surged from a gap in the cliff, guided by two tribesmen in traditional clothes, their weapons slung across their backs. Am Hussein handed the lamb to Hikmat and then, aslant the wind, moved towards the tribesmen, his arms opening slowly: a hawk spreading its wings. Click. Then a black knight embracing two warriors. Click. Hikmat and Abla followed him. Nader tugged at my arm as we trailed along behind. 'I'm flying, Koko!' he crowed.

'One little push and you'll be flying for real.'

'You won't. Too many witnesses.'

'You think a bunch of outlaws would defend your case?'

'Touché,' he chuckled. To his credit, he loves a good point made, even if it's against himself.

The caravan was now making a U-turn. Am Hussein mounted one mule. Abla sat sideways on another behind him. She secured her hair with her flowery shawl but the wind was threatening to unpettle its flowers. Sadly, it was another click I couldn't take. The tribesmen, their weapons held high, shouted Hala! and plunged down the gorge on foot. Hikmat instructed Nader to bend his leg, then cradled his foot and hauled him up into the saddle. The Maestro sat ramrod straight, smirking at me: 'I told you the Samurai are coming!'

I copied Am Hussein, gripping the pommel, inserting my left foot into the stirrup and lifting my body up in one thrust.

I felt vulnerable and wobbly but the animal gave no cause for concern.

We lined up and began the terrifying descent down the narrow gorge. I'd never ridden a mule before. I held the reins with one hand and clutched the pommel with the other, clasping my legs around the animal's belly. The precipitous path made me cringe. Not Nader. He took the hellish descent theatrically, talking gibberish to a mule that had never grazed hashish or been ridden by an ersatz Samurai. Covering his panic? It was comedy and drama rolled into one.

Suddenly I glimpsed a white mass flapping on top of the cliff. At the same time a shrapnel of pebbles shot out from under my mule's hoofs, causing it to stumble. It jerked its neck up and then down. I lurched backward, holding the reins steady with both hands, and just managed to reinstate my bum on the saddle.

'What's that?' I called to Hikmat, pointing upwards.

'That's her.'

'The bride?'

'No, the white witch.'

'Coming to the wedding?'

'Who knows – she's as unpredictable as a scorpion.'

'You don't like her, do you?'

'Sure I do. I'm taking her donkey to the vet later today.'

The path was almost vertical. I couldn't keep chatting to Hikmat without risking a fall, but I made a mental note to find out more about that woman.

Just before we reached the foot of the cliff, the ground began to level. The animals snorted and shook their heads. I was secure enough in the saddle now to look up. She was gone. I scanned the blue dome. She appeared again above the mouth of the waterfall, seeming to float like a white cloud. I clamped my knees firmly on my mount, took my camera and focused on the cliff. She was gone again. Now you see me now you don't. Was she playing with us?

We dismounted. Stepping onto the ground felt odd, as if I had shrunk. My inner thighs cried fire. My scrotum ached. Bow-legged, I delivered my mule back to the tribesmen: Ahmad, brother of the bride, and Wajeeh, brother of the groom. We shook hands. They tethered all the mules to wooden poles and escorted us to our designated tent. Like all of them, it had an open frontage and was made of multicoloured patches like a quilt. The floor was covered with straw mats and lined with cushions. There were trays of dates and loukoum and baklavas, and trays of fruit – mainly mandarins, oranges and bananas – spread on small tables, neatly arranged. The aroma of vegetables stewed in spices filtered through the canvas from the adjacent tent, foretelling an imminent banquet. I was starving. Abla went to the neighbouring tent and came back with a tray of tea and almonds. She seemed more carefree away from home. Her smile revealed a woman attuned to herself, a swan confident on her own river, as if the whole place was hers. This mysterious woman puzzled me more and more, but one can't just toss out a personal query concerning a local female out here. It would be crossing the line. Nonetheless, I gestured with my head for Hikmat to follow me outside. He obliged.

'Just out of curiosity, OK? What did Abla do before? I mean when she was married to your uncle, God bless his soul?'

'When the bride comes, have a look at her dress. Abla made it.'

'So she's a dressmaker?'

'Specialist, only for brides. She even went to Italy to show some Italian designer how to embroider with beads, Bedouin style.'

People were trickling to the tents from every direction out of the surrounding mountains. Some came on foot, others on mules, horses, and donkeys, gathering in small groups before filtering into their tents. The children mostly clustered round their mothers, while the men congregated, lighting up and chatting. Many had their weapons conspicuously on their shoulders. Others slung them on to their backs.

Outside, the sun was strikingly bright, no shade in the barren land around us. The only trees were the short sturdy junipers growing in crevices on the rocky slopes. They looked forbidding, like sentinels.

It was time for the sacrifice. Am Hussein tried to convince Nader to come and watch but Nader declined and slunk away. I knew how much he hated blood and so didn't interfere. The lamb seemed resigned to its fate as our little procession carried it to the foot of the waterfall. It knew the end was nigh and was mustering whatever courage a victim can muster in such circumstances. When the executioners crouched to turn its head towards Mecca, it was hopeless trying to shoot them against the powerful glare. I needed a higher position, so I climbed a little way up the rugged slope. I clicked the three men – Wajeeh, Ahmad and Am Hussein – bending over the lamb. Then the flicker of the knife's blade and the water clouding with blood. Only a tiny part of the lamb, all fluffy and white, was visible between the looming bulk of their dark clothes. I could see it coming good in black and white. But I needed more. I climbed a little further, hoping to include a wider scene. To my surprise, there was Nader, lying on his back, arms spread like a crucifix on a wide stone ledge, gazing at a cloud. 'Nader, you're looking like shit.'

'I'm in that cloud, Koko.'

'Are you coming down?'

'How can one eat one's own flesh? That lamb was me; you know. Listen, his requiem.'

Through the silence seeped a melody from Yousef's flute, though there was no sign of the shepherd or his flock.

'Our hosts will be offended if you don't honour their hospitality. Come on.'

'O God! God! How weary, stale, flat and unprofitable seem to me all the uses of this world . . . '

Nader the schizophrenic, popping in and out of all his delusions. Anything to avoid being pinned down to reality. Exasperated, I tried a dose of plain speaking: 'Nader, Nishan walked his first steps today, Burhan Sadik lost his only daughter, the country is remembering the second anniversary of the civil war. And you, where are you?'

'I am dead Horatio. Wretched Queen, adieu!
                            . . . O! I die, Horatio.'

In the end I called Am Hussein. He came up, took a long look at Nader and smiled. Then he grabbed him by his belt and lifted him like a bag of sawdust. Nader flailed around, demanding to be left alone. 'We shed blood in your honour and you hide like a rabbit?' Am Hussein was half-angry, half-teasing. To his credit, Nader stopped fighting and began laughing. My shot of the satisfied hunter hefting his catch was a gem.

I ache with yearning for my son and for the soothing presence of my wife. Arsiné, I know I am not eloquent with loving words, but I am sure you hear my heartbeats. When was the last time I ate away from home with such a burning desire to have you near me? Grab a sandwich and run, Koko, eat while running, while breathing the acrid smell of the dark room, while crouching in the most unappetising corners of incinerated Beirut. Eat to fuel your run, anything, anywhere, anytime. 'What is this we're eating?' Emile asked one day. I didn't know either. We were counting the whistles of bullets, taking shelter from a sniper. We weren't hungry. But we ate something like cardboard just the same.

Today I know what I'm eating. I've seen my food alive. The little creature with misty eyes looked like the lamb in Jesus' arms. Only he wasn't saved but sacrificed for our own salvation. And now he's melting in my mouth, dispatching to the far ends of my mind the tang of unfamiliar herbs. Its fleece is hanging to dry from the branch of a nearby juniper. Its head and entrails have been put in a basin to be cleaned and cooked later, stuffed with rice and spices. Neck, shank, shoulder, breast, loin, legs and ribs, all spread on a large tin, letting the sizzling fat drip into the stream. The high heat method is best for young lambs, Hikmat said. It brings out the flavour and gives it a good crust. Yum! I feel as if I am munching with your jaws, Arsiné, and smiling as you do when you like your food. I love that smile. It floods your eyes with enchantment. It goes back to when we used to get together for lunch, savouring the spicy cooking of Aunty Clauda, sitting at the table overlooking the busy street where cart-pushing vendors shouted their goods. You'd look at me and beam that smile. We'd clean the plates of Borali, and Itsh, and Suberek, and collapse for a doze in the living room. Aunty Clauda couldn't refuse you the moon if you asked for it because she considered you my saviour. She also felt it as a compliment, seeing you appreciate her cooking with that special smile. Love isn't always red roses and serenades in the moonlight. It can also be eating in a derelict street where children and adults seem to be having an eternal screaming match and the sun's rays are as rare as the torch flash of a lazy watchman.

I wish Nishan was here, in this open wilderness, toddling about, touching dirt and water, going wherever he wants, hearing nothing but the wind, feeling it through his hair, smelling the scent of the mountains. The thought of him living out his childhood confined to the dreary walls of an apartment hurts me more than death. Remember the day we took him to the gardens of Zouk, how he sat there, squinting, all white in the sunlight, his little body drowned in the blades of grass? We didn't know why he wasn't responding to our calls. 'Come on, Neesh, let's play ball, come on now!' We rolled the red rubber ball towards him, but he ignored it. It took us a while to realise that our son was being exposed for the first time to the texture of soil and grass. He was patting it with a comical mixture of apprehension and delight. Poor soul, he was growing up in a concrete jungle, never venturing further than another cement block at your parents' or my uncle's – ceasefires permitting, of course. Fuck the Pasha. And fuck the militias. And fuck this war for depriving children of their childhood.

Arsiné!

How would you like a wedding picnic with some outlaws, huh? You'd love these near-biblical characters, these hard-core men living their own chosen destiny with a philosophy that defies logic and challenges reason. I'm savouring with these men the nuance between eating and feasting. And I am happy. And I am sad – if only I could share this moment with you. It's not the smoke, for I only had a few puffs, and of course good Muslims don't drink or serve alcohol. I suppose it must be the fresh, fresh air. So fresh that if you close your eyes you're reduced to ether. And the sound of distance, all those melodious ripples like a mirage of ancient pilgrims caravanning across a belt of hills. I'll bet you Mount Ararat feels the same. If only one day the gods would waft us up there, Arsiné. We could repair Noah's ark and start a new breed of Armenians free from the wounds of the past.

12

I took some of my best shots at the waterfall, the men washing their hands and faces after the meal while Abla handed down a bar of homemade soap and a towel. The position of these tough men crouching at her feet, and the solemn and dignified expression on her face, gave an almost religious aspect to the scene. When I managed to frame her profile alone my heart leapt to my throat as she gave a faint smile of collaboration.

We were still sipping our after-lunch tea when Nader took one of his deep yogi breaths. Spreading his arms slightly, he hushed the casual conversation with a formal opening: 'I am Nader Abi Nader, and my colleague here is Krikor Krikorian, the famous Koko. The *Daily Sun* has sent us to cover this wedding and to hear about your plan to end the civil war.' The information was laid down with digital precision, as if he were sending a wired message to a remote continent. Then he produced the newspaper cutting and translated it in that same lofty tone. I felt embarrassed for him. No one in Lebanon is unaware of traditional Arab hospitality. You wait to state the purpose of your visit until asked. Besides, you don't break the general mood with a pompous declaration like that.

Am Hussein brought his palm to his forehead and smiled. 'The wedding starts soon,' he said. 'It's not an ordinary wedding. It's a ceremony of reconciliation between all the feuding tribes in the valley. Many hatchets will be buried today. Meanwhile, we can use the remaining time to listen to brother Wajeeh and perhaps also brother Ahmad. Their reflections, especially on their time behind bars, may provide a few thoughts about how to end this war.'

Wajeeh was taken by surprise. So far he hadn't said much. He'd eaten in silence and been the first to finish. His pyramidal Adam's apple shifted nervously beneath the skin of his sturdy neck even before he started to speak. He opened his palms upward in a gesture of detached assent. There was a strong sense of fatalism in this prelude. Click.

'We may seem a curiosity to you city people,' he began, overcoming his shyness at last. 'Yes, we have our vendettas, but our social and moral traditions are far more civilised than your savage war and your decadent peace.' Now he looked sharply at Nader. 'You must know and write that, Ustaz Nader. There has never been a thief in any respectable tribe around here. Never did any of us kill another in a sectarian brawl. We don't have those shameful brawls anyway. And we don't wait in the dark for a Christian to wander by and stab him in the back or shoot him and his family just because they happen to be Christians. We see and hear what's going on in this war. Families dragged out of their beds, slaughtered blindly. This is a return to animal behaviour. What am I saying? Animals never sink that low.'

His expression as well as his words projected an unnecessary defensiveness. He was introducing not only himself but a fact of life bigger than himself. 'I did shoot someone. I'm not sorry. On the contrary, I'm proud of it. A man is not a man who walks with his head weighed down by shame. One day my father was mocked in public. An old man can become forgetful. It's normal. He was ninety-three, still strong in his body, but he would become confused and sometimes lose his way. One day a young bum called Fadel showed him the wrong direction home, just for fun, and got him completely lost. We waited for him for dinner. We went to every house in the village looking for him, including Fadel's who denied seeing him. The whole village joined us. We took flashlights and dogs and fanned out, covering the whole area. Four days later we found him, in a ditch in the middle of a hemp field, miles from home, sleeping like a child. When we woke him up his tears welled. No one had ever seen my father cry. It was hard on everyone, especially my mother. Later he remembered who had played this prank. We went to Fadel's parents and told them what had happened. They were very sorry. His father ordered him to go kiss my father's hand and ask his forgiveness. But the bum was too proud to do it. His father kicked him out. He took off to Sidon, hid himself in the Palestinian camp of Ain Helweh, and boasted about the senile git he'd led into the wilderness. A few months later he showed up in a paramilitary jeep with two hooded fighters. He was standing behind a machine gun, shamelessly showing off. I was in my shop. I loaded my rifle and called him. 'Fadel,' I cried, 'Are you going to kiss my father's hand?' He turned around laughing, pointing the big gun at me. So I shot him dead.'

The Adam's apple stopped its journey up and down Wajeeh's throat. Am Hussein's face was blank. 'Thank you, brother Wajeeh. But what can we gather from this unfortunate incident?'

'If Fadel hadn't found refuge and back-up elsewhere, he wouldn't have been able to challenge his own people,' Wajeeh said matter-of-factly.

'So . . . alliance with anyone against your own is treason,' Am Hussein concluded.

Wajeeh nodded, clutching his jaw. It seemed easier for him to tell the story than to extract wisdom from it.

Am Hussein drew on his nargileh and puffed out a cone of white smoke. 'That's good, Brother Wajeeh. Now tell us how it was for you inside. Remember the way you described life at the Raml prison? Tell our guests about it, if you don't mind.'

Wajeeh gave a wistful grin. He lowered his head thoughtfully. In my lens his furrowed brow resembled ridges seen from an aeroplane. He took a noisy sip of his tea, shifted his position and began by describing the Kawoosh, where up to eighty prisoners lived together, of all religions and all sects, along with a few foreigners. They ate together, sharing any food brought from outside. 'Because, you see, the prison food was served in a bucket and smelled of rot – we automatically threw it into the toilet. So sharing our food was customary. There were some poor buggers who had no one in the world to bring them food, and there were some rich buggers who managed to indulge us with first-class banquets. It levelled up nicely. No sectarian frictions. And I mean none. Each group kept together to sleep and pray, but at dawn we gathered our mats, piled them by the wall and mingled. There were no boundaries to friendships. Bonding with inmates from different sects was normal, and some of these bonds became as deep as blood relations.'

Nader was smiling all over his face, shaking his head in wonder. 'Marvellous!'

'How is it marvellous, Ustaz Nader?' Am Hussein queried.

'Confinement as a transcendantal condition. It makes people realise their priorities and live the best they can. We need walls to enclose our whole country rather than fences around each sect, so we learn to need each other rather than rely on foreign handouts. Self-sufficiency. Once we throw the smelly bucket of division down the toilet we live happily ever after.'

Am Hussein was pleased. 'We couldn't have put it better.' He took a long self-congratulatory puff and added earnestly, 'But how are we to put this dream into action when everyone is killing everyone else, Ustaz Nader?'

'We kill sectarianism instead,' Nader said.

'We're getting there,' replied Am Hussein, shaking Nader's hand and keeping it in his grip. 'Is sectarianism a lamb or wolf, in your opinion, sir?'

Nader winced at the vigour of Am Hussein's grip, but he wasn't lost for words. He ventured the popular proverb: 'If you are not a wolf, the wolves will eat you.'

'We'll settle for that for now,' Am Hussein laughed, freeing Nader's crumpled little hand.

Spontaneously, we all lifted our tea glasses in a cheerful toast.

Now it was Ahmad's turn to seduce my lens: puffy nose, moustache drooping like the blades of Yemeni daggers, and jade green eyes. His silent countenance radiated decency, a sense of inner wealth. He brought to mind my uncle's words: 'Some people come and go like clouds, you don't register them. They're shadows, faceless ghosts. Others you know at first sight will stick in your memory for as long as you have one.' Ahmad seemed like one of those. I moved around him, clicking away while Nader took notes.

'My father, unlike Wajeeh's, was not a very good man.' Ahmad made no attempt to soften the shame of this declaration. He lowered his gaze and cleared his throat. 'It's a fact. He had a reputation for being honest and God-fearing, but he wasn't. He kept his vengeance steaming in his chest for fifteen years, all the while pretending forgiveness. You see, in a hunting accident my eldest brother had been shot dead by the son of Hajj Abbas, a very powerful tribal leader, as you probably know. My father refused apologies and money. He said no money or words could ever compensate for his son. Yet he refrained from seeking reprisal. He just hid his grief for fifteen years. Then one day he drove his old Chevy across the Bekaa to Sehmur, where the Hajj's only grandson, just turned sixteen, was tending a vineyard . . . '

Ahmad stopped, his face troubled. He seemed to be fighting an army of words, unable to find the right ones. But I could picture all too well what had happened: a geriatric, hardened by prolonged grief, taking his vengeance on an innocent teenager. Ahmad conveyed all this with his tumultuous silence. Then he continued, 'My father drove back to Zahleh and gave himself up. But that's like paying an onion peel for an ounce of gold, like hiding from the coming storm behind your own shadow. Something drastic, something to fit the inevitable reaction, had to be done. You don't kill the only grandson of a man as important as the Hajj without reprisals. Hiding my old man in prison would only add insult to injury. My other brother was whisked away from Lebanon immediately. As I was the only target left at large, the gendarmes sent for me. Our village elders came at night to visit us. They asked my mother to make tea, which at that hour signals that this is between men only. She knew what would happen. She didn't make tea. She went to her room and cried her eyes out. They drove me to Zahleh. This sort of negotiation is always done in strictest secrecy. We sat on the floor of a solitary confinement cell: my father, me, two elders, and Zahleh's police chief. They used a horrible brew of coercion and law enforcement and tribal history and political affiliations and personal connections and emotional blackmail to force me to take the rap. "Let your father off the hook. It's more honourable and will ease the fury of your enemies to know that one day they might have the chance to kill you."

'Most shocking of all, my father consented. "There's no shame in doing a stretch in prison," he said. "We'll work something out for you. Now that your brother's blood has been avenged, we are on the same level as the Hajj." He was so casual about it. My own life was no more than a link in a long bloody chain.' Ahmad's tone remained steady, like early morning waves. 'What do I do? Say no, I'm not going to prison for a crime I didn't commit and have my father put behind bars, at his age? Anyway, I was already there, already incarcerated. Any chance of escape had been cut off. What looked like a meeting to "find a solution" was in reality a verdict of life in prison. I was twenty, in my second year of study to become a dentist. I was so numb with surprise my mind kept repeating, this is not happening, not happening –'

'Just a second, brother Ahmad,' Nader interrupted. 'You had

to sign an admission of guilt. I mean, they had to have you sign something for the record. What did they write? Did they make up a totally different story or what?'

'Once a deal is sealed the papers come and go like nothing. I did read my own confession before signing. It simply cited my full name, the date of the murder, and that I did it to avenge my brother. They have a set formula for such confessions; all you do is fill in the form.'

'But what if you refused, said you wanted to speak to a lawyer, what then?'

Nader's law school remark caused great merriment. Even Abla broke her silence: 'Hire a lawyer and prepare to die,' she said, and covered her mouth with the tail of her scarf.

'But how could a professional lawyer harm your case?' Nader went on, regardless.

'Lawyers work for money,' Ahmad said. 'Time is their money machine. The longer a case drags on through the courts, the more money they make. Whereas the understanding established between authorities and tribes cuts legalities to a minimum. In all the history of Lebanese vendettas, no one has been hanged, nor has anyone stayed behind bars for more than a few years. That's far better than any lawyer could achieve. In this way at least, the law has been lenient to us. Before the war there was hope that more education and integration into society would gradually make vendettas a thing of the past. Now . . . well, the whole country is a killing field.'

Large blue veins stood out on Nader's forehead. 'So let me get this right. You went to prison. You were given a sentence of how many years?'

'Life.'

'Life?'

'Yes. At least, that's the sentence on paper, for the general public. But the minute I entered Raml, bargaining for my conditional release started behind the scenes. It was 1957.

Unfortunately, less than a year later the insurgence of '58 began. And after that President Chehab came to power. Everything froze. Then, as soon as mediations began again there was the coup of '61. I tell you, luck was not smiling on me.' A rueful smile flickered in Ahmad's eyes. 'My father died in '62. Despite everything, I cried for him. Fellow inmates advised me to ask for a retrial then, tell it as it happened. Instead, I wrote a letter to the President. I told him the truth, not asking for favours or clemency, just stating the facts. It was a short letter. I still have a copy.' Ahmad reached into his jacket. Nader held out his hand eagerly. He took the brown piece of paper, obviously cut from a grocery bag, and read it aloud:

'Excellency, I was studying to become a dentist. I killed no one. I had to say that I did to protect my father. He lived by the ancient rule of tribal vendettas. I beg you to help put an end to this horrible tradition so that no other innocent young men will become outlaws and waste their lives. This is God's honest truth, may He bless you and inspire your decisions.'

It was uncharacteristic of level-headed cold-blooded General Chehab to be moved by a few lines from a prisoner. But his powerful intelligence service, the fearsome Second Bureau, presented him with a report confirming Ahmad's story. He ordered his release.

A big smile lit Ahmad's face. 'It was a beautiful day. Every day since has been a beautiful day. Sure, I've had to give up my dentistry studies and live out here hidden from the hired guns of Hajj Abbas. But being free is everything – not just from the prison walls, but from the tribe and its suffocating norms. And now from the civil war.'

For me, the raw data wasn't enough. I was dying to know what it had felt like, being punished for the sins of your father, how he could have cried when the bastard died. He had lost his dream and part of his youth for what?

'From university to Raml. How did you cope?' I asked.

'I was lucky in prison. When I went to Raml I was sent to the Kawoosh governed by Garo.' Ahmad gave me a knowing glance. 'Garo took me under his wing. He brought me to sleep near him and made me his deputy. Newcomers usually slept near the shit hole and were made to serve the others. So when Garo was released I became boss. I'm not exaggerating when I tell you that I was king in Raml, even though the kingdom was not of my choosing.'

Am Hussein looped his arm round Ahmad's neck and kissed his forehead. His words were laden with sudden emotion: 'You are the only one, the one and only, ya Ahmad.' The only outlaw who hadn't killed anybody? The one with the answer to Nader's quest? I looked at Nader, hoping he'd follow up, but his last joint had finally caught up with him and his notebook lay abandoned.

At this altitude the sun had warmed us just enough, but now the northerly was grating chunks of snow from the higher peaks and the breeze was getting cooler by the minute. Nader's chest was wheezing audibly. I feared an asthma attack but knew that warning him would trigger the opposite reaction; he would be angry, asking for more pot.

Am Hussein noticed. I think he also sensed my concern. He turned to Hikmat. 'Bring him a cloak.' To Abla he said, 'A spoonful of honey in some hot tea, my soul.'

Before he knew it, a woollen abaya was covering Nader's body like the hump of a camel, leaving only his head exposed. The cup of tea completed the picture of a universal hobo.

'Brother Ahmad, your story is very touching. What can we deduce from it today in your opinion?' I said, knowing that I wasn't very good at this.

'Oh, I'm sorry.' Ahmad clasped his fingers together as if in prayer. 'I thought it was obvious: we need a firm but merciful government. Chehab might have been oppressive in some ways but he held the country together. After him it began to fall apart, don't you think?'

So much for the 'solution' for ending the war.

I nodded, concealing my disappointment.

13

Our little party was breaking up. Ahmad and Wajeeh said their farewells and left. Soon after, Abla touched her husband's shoulder gently, inclined her neck and whispered something in his ear. Then she waved goodbye to us and strolled towards a tent crowded with women. A flash of colour caressed by the breeze fluttering over a green plateau. Click. Click. I smuggled the smuggler's wife again into my lens. Although shot from the back, it evoked in me a feeling akin to the first stirrings of romance.

Hikmat leaned towards my ear: 'She's gone to help dress the bride.'

'Is she coming back?'

'Later,' Hikmat said.

I loaded my camera and fitted in a wide angle, ready for group clicks.

Not long after Abla disappeared into the ladies tent, the thudding of drums – bou-boum . . . bou-boum . . . bou-boum – announced the beginning of the ceremony. The men all loaded their guns and held them high above their heads. Today, guns as adornment, pride and status. But guns nonetheless.

The drum roll paved the way for two swordsmen, one from each side of the green, clad in black sherwals, white collarless shirts and high riding boots, wielding real Arabian swords and small engraved metal shields. Their faces were hidden in red keffias, their eyes fiercely focused. They approached the centre with simulated threats and bold leaps. It was a dance of calculated steps and movements, with little if any improvisation. The choreography reflected a balance of danger and play, even humour from time to time when a trap was cleverly escaped. The audience clapped, hup . . . hup . . . hup, simulating a believable confrontation. The duellists picked up on the rhythm and began their defying twirls. In a series of wind-whipping, sky-slashing, ghost-stabbing manoeuvres, they tackled each other. The vast space around us began to shrink. All attention was narrowed on them. Blades brushed against shields sounding like tin bells. Near-misses were combined with airy acrobatics, making the threat of serious injury seem imminent. The audience held its breath in unison. The drums celebrated each major stunt. Up close, the wielding of sabres was more exciting than the actual clashes. The spectacular jumps and rolls were each hurrahed. The audience knew there would be no injuries, so they egged the swordsmen on to fan the air faster and faster with their swords. I was clicking away, keeping enough distance not to obstruct the game or the sightlines. The duellists ended face to face, crossing blades and banging their shields. A few zealots emptied their pistols in the air. The duellists crossed their swords together one last time, high above their heads, and bowed to their audience. Rounds of gunfire fractured the blue dome, rose petals rained down on the combatants as finally they uncovered their faces to reveal none other than Wajeeh and Ahmad.

Who would have guessed?

As they walked away from the centre, the crowd thickened by the tents. Heads bobbed, gazes switched from one side of the green to the other. A new expectation was mounting. Then a powerful drum roll sounded and two cavalry divisions in full tribal attire surged from east and west of the green. 'Hheeeey!' The crowd saluted as twelve men on each side, sporting old German and English rifles, formed lines facing each other. The drums rose in a crescendo. The horses were eager to go. They pawed the ground with their hooves and tossed their heads impatiently, but their riders remained calm and centred. Then a shot rang out and they charged at full gallop towards each other, hooves ploughing the green. At the meeting point the men raised their weapons to the sky and let out a barrage of fire as the two lines filtered through each other to opposite sides. Again the drums, again the charge, again the shots, seven times, until the cheering overrode even the thudding munitions and the air reeked of cordite.

After the last charge the cavalry formed a circle around the perimeter of the green. Then the guns were lowered and the sweaty, snorting horses were taken to rest.

Next, the drummers and the flautists began to play the compelling rhythm of a Dabkeh. Dozens of people came together holding hands, forming a large semi-circle, leaving the middle free for the solo performers and for those who wished to sing a few verses.

> Oh dear bride save the pearls of your tears
> For later. Go on to live, enjoy the happy years
> Take a moment alone at your window sill
> And pray may everyone marry as their hearts will
> Lee, lee, lee.

This from an old woman: eyes closed, mouth toothless, wave upon wave of years rippling across her tawny brow. Her soft throaty voice delighted everyone, bringing a refreshing tenderness to the scene.

The Dabkeh stopped, a sharp silence cutting off the staccato rhythms. This was the moment everyone was waiting for. A procession was coming from the eastern side of the enclave, three drummers heading it. The women, carrying trays of rose petals, started their tongue-rattling ululation. Other musicians blew their double-reed flutes. And behind them came a crowd of men, women and children, a fractured rainbow rolling on to the green. In their midst, a black stallion aflutter with yellow ribbons and little copper bells held the bride. A sunburst of golden beads twinkled on her white muslin dress. Abla's signature was all over it, a taste of refined authenticity.

A second procession was emerging from the western side. The same formation of drummers and flautists, but this time a white mare adorned with red ribbons, ridden by the groom resplendent in a black abaya embroidered with silver threads. As the two groups met in the middle of the green, a loud collective Hala! rose into the air. A volley of gunfire answered it and the women showered the sky with rose petals. Then the two processions angled off in opposite directions. The nuptial horses moved towards the centre. The bride's face remained veiled until she was a short distance from her groom. Then she lifted the veil. Women ululated. The groom circled around her a few times, never taking his eyes off her. He was wooing her in a show of chivalry, asserting the ancient male supremacy with style and finesse. There was no need for words. This was basic, visceral and seductive. Then, abruptly, he swept her on to his saddle and galloped off towards the western exit amidst a final hail of gunfire.

Century after century these people would retain their authenticity. Even now, in the middle of a savage civil war, in the middle of this barren landscape, a tribal 'republic' was celebrating a princely wedding to revive their links and express solidarity in the face of nationwide disintegration. Perhaps Am Hussain was right after all; maybe these 'outlaws' did hold the key to stopping the Lebanese fratricides.

The formal part of the wedding was over. Everyone began mingling, embracing, exchanging babies from arm to arm. The children to-ed and fro-ed, their limbs whirling like coloured fans. They were released at last and reclaiming their territory with gusto. I imagined Nishan among them and I clicked away with renewed enthusiasm. The children were more than willing to pose. They laughed, clustered tightly together as if the lens might blow them away. I had anticipated three rolls and kept two for emergencies. Now I was nearing the end of my last roll. The thought of running out of film was as scary as a deaf man bereft of his hearing aid. I hoped Nader might have a roll in his jacket – occasionally he manages to think like a professional – so I went back to the tent. It was empty. Flies and wasps had found the leftovers and were having their own wedding feast. Outside was a crowd of strangers. I scanned them carefully but couldn't see Nader or Hikmat or anyone else from Dyarna. My desire for more clicks ebbed. I tucked my camera in my bag, ready to leave. I had enough clicks for two stories. I could tell Fathy what the outlaws had said about the war – an anecdote worth a few lines to justify the photos – and the wedding clicks would delight his love of contrast: a sumptuous wedding to offset the thousands of low-profile funerals.

I waved goodbye to the children and walked to where the mules had been tied. They were gone too. The steep descent on a mule had been ordeal enough. Climbing back up on foot with my gear through that near-vertical scar in the rocky gorge was out of the question.

'Looking for me?' It was Hikmat.

'Have you seen Nader?'

'Over there,' he said, pointing.

Nader was, as expected, getting stoned. He sat on the ground smoking a Goza made of coconut shell and thin reed. He was attracting an audience of curious onlookers. His eyes were at half-mast, his lips flaccid, his jaw slack.

'Have a puff, Koko.'

'What are you smoking, man?'

'Opium cocktail.'

'Yeah?'

'Ye . . . ah.'

'You're looking like a mummy.'

'I have to finish Pirate, Koko. It's happening. Draw a puff with me. We don't need the Baddours. Just you and me.'

He was completely in thrall to his vision, looking at me but far beyond me, as if the crew and the camera and the sea were all there. Worse still, he'd convinced himself that I, of all people, was going to help him shoot his virtual Pirate. It was pathetically funny. I burst out laughing. The crowd copied me uncertainly. A cold wind whipped us from the west. I scowled at the strangers. They shuffled away, hissing like a pack of vampires. I bent down near Nader. In moments like this I hated him pure and simple. Had I a gun I might have put a bullet in his fucked-up head and watched the kernels of his baked brains erupting like popcorn.

'Koko,' he said, pointing east, 'Only Samurai come from the window of the sun; pirates are just spat out by the waves. I want a slow travelling, your widest angle. I want the blades of grass and the highest clouds together as if inside a cocoon. Trust me, my friend. I know,' he assured me, pointing at his pulsating temple.

I brought my nose to his.

'There's no one there, dickhead. Toshiro Mifune left the Samurai. Actually, they kicked his silly ass out because they found your face printed on his underwear. And if you don't move your butt now, we'll be left alone in this place. No, you'll be left alone. I'm going back to my woman and my son. I have to drop by the grocer, I have to check on my uncle, I have to pay my condolences to my boss and I have to take a shower. This is the last shot of Pirate, Nader: Koko taking a shower. Read: The End.'

His eyes froze. 'It's over then?'

'It's over.'

I don't know what snapped inside him, but tears seeped out and trickled into his beard. For once there were no histrionics. He had vacated his face, leaving only a motionless mask, but his welling eyes were still fixed on me. 'I dedicate Pirate to the only woman who didn't hate me: my mother,' he murmured.

'Fine. Let's hope she'll forgive you for killing her. Come on.'

I put my hands under his armpits and lifted him to his feet. He felt spongy-dry, fragile. I feared he would collapse, so I folded him across my shoulder like a rolled-up rug. He was light. His breathing was erratic, sounding like broken hail on a tin roof. Every now and then he mumbled something inaudible. Was he delirious? Or just acting. Maybe impersonating a wounded Napoleonic general at the Russian front being led to a live burial in a snow-filled ditch. Or maybe he was kneeling at Iwona's feet, begging her to forgive him: 'I'm so sorry my love, for I have been a selfish bastard. Allow me to wash your feet with my tears!' Or maybe, at long last, he was coming to terms with his terrifying manslaughter of his mother – reverse gear at the wrong moment plus a fitful snap of fury and there she was, splattered all over the garage wall still clasping his sandwich. On the other hand, he could be replaying the film of his botched-up life. All those years with Grotowsky, learning a language he will never use again, playing in shows that will never be seen again, and fathering a child who will never call him Dad. Then coming back to a homeland on the brink of disintegration and crying out, To be or not to be. Like Hamlet, he was leaving behind a trail of death and destruction, not a happy kingdom.

Uncle Varouj once told me, 'If you help someone you would rather kill, consider the deed done.' It was true. Having Nader at my mercy felt good. I could do what I liked with him now: dump him in a ditch or abandon him in the middle of the green, a tasty snack for the hyenas. Yet isn't it strange, how Life itself has value, regardless of who owns it? Am I making sense here? Or am I just trying to justify why I was carrying my arch enemy and beginning to fear for his life, while still harbouring the desire to snuff that life out?

The sleek black stallion that had carried the bride surged from the gap between the eastern mountains in a smooth gallop, seemingly riderless. Then Hikmat's head popped up from behind its neck. 'Hey!' he yelled. 'Where are you taking Hamlet?' Where indeed? I spun round to call him but he was already turning the horse. He dismounted in one neat jump, still holding the bridle. 'Is he dead?'

'Yes.' Nader's voice issued from the vicinity of my coccyx.

'Well, a burial after a wedding isn't so bad,' Hikmat said cheerfully, gesturing me to throw Nader across the saddle.

The stallion was tall and twitchy. Hikmat was clutching its bridle and trying to calm the beast. Meanwhile Nader continued to assert his demise. I had to lift him like a sacrifice. Maybe he was dying. Only a near-corpse would consent to dangle like that, unconcerned about the hooves of a restless stallion.

His breath changed to a continuous gurgle. It scared me. 'This isn't working,' I said to Hikmat, 'He'll choke to death like this.'

'So you don't want to finish the movie?'

'Come on, give me a hand.'

'I can't let go of the bridle. He'll take off.'

'Wrap the reins round your wrist, they're long enough. Come on, please.'

'I thought we were shooting a movie. Nader said we were.'

'Yeah? Where's the camera?'

'You!'

'Is that what Nader told you.'

'Sure. He said, "Take a puff and work with me. Go get your horse, my Samurai," he said.'

'Come here!' I barked.

Hikmat finally got the message and helped me lay Nader down.

Nader's skin felt rubbery. I knelt beside him and rubbed his hands. 'Where's your father?' I asked Hikmat.

'With the others, clearing up.'

'Go tell him we need to take Nader to hospital. Don't just stand there – go!'

Hikmat climbed onto his stallion and galloped away.

The light dimmed as the sun sank behind the mountains. The green lost its freshness, became harder. The last caravan of laden mules was crossing the green, led by a solitary old man. I cupped Nader's hands in mine, rubbed them and warmed them with my breath. His fingers were frozen blue, turning white and puffy. My efforts had little effect. His eyes were floating in and out. His tongue stirred a fraction – he wants to speak? For once I was eager to hear anything he had to say, just to hear his voice surface and see his morbidly dry lips move. If it weren't for the faint wheezing of his chest and the occasional flutter of his eyelids, I might have pronounced him dead and walked away. But he had to die first. To die or not to die, was the crucial question today. And regardless of how much I wished he had never been born, I didn't want him to die, not now for God's sake.

A sudden gush of sadness climbed my throat. Aunty Clauda's voice swam up through my memory: 'When you're young, you're naïve enough to imagine a third path, another end to the farce. But no, Koko, time will show you how pitiful we are, how helpless when this heap of flesh and water betrays us. And what cowards we are. We hang on to the last breath of life even if drowning in our own shit, even if nothing is working any more but the mere inhaling and exhaling.'

I loved Aunty Clauda's no-nonsense views on most things, but this image of utter helplessness had put the fear of God in me. Now it was all unfolding before me. Nader was barely breathing, bubbling like a water pipe. With each weak intake of air he battled the dwindling shreds of his fading life, sucking me into his fight. I held him tight and cried out, 'Come on, Maestro, I thought we were going to find out how to end this war.'

To my surprise, he opened his eyes, noted my presence and heaved a long, scratchy jet of air: 'It's not what you find, Koko, but what finds you.' His voice was thin but his breath was beginning to kick in again. 'This time the wolf is coming for real. Wave after wave, my felucca is drawing closer to the final shore. Give me your hand, my friend.'

I gave him my hand. He held it with a fierce grip, as if holding on to life itself. Then he sighed. 'Death's not as bad as it sounds, Koko,' he said. 'The slate is wiped clean, the sins are forgiven. One is washed and embalmed and even the asthmatics breathe freely.' He lowered his gaze, letting a wan smile filter into his face. 'Death is great, Koko. It's the everlasting break into the zone of perfect lighting. It's deliverance from this wretched waiting state.' His eyelids flicked like little wings. 'We're all wretched one way or another, Koko. Don't believe otherwise. No artist, no creative mind is free from wretchedness. Forget the gloss of success and fame, scratch the surface and you'll find a miserable wretch beneath. Only perpetual, unconditional, unhindered creativity saves us. The more you create the hungrier you get for more. It's when you're idle and grounded that death finds you and takes you.'

Then he opened his eyes widely and tilted his head towards the mountains. 'You know what, Koko?' His face lit up. 'Let's film Death in Lapland, what do you say? Imagine long shots from those sleds drawn by huskies. Bright luminous shots showing the deception of time through the awesome midnight sun. Day and night embracing, warmth and ice fusing. Millions, trillions of shadows fleeing across the slopes as we drive on to embrace the source of life. We see no flesh, we hear no sound except perhaps Bach's organ rising slowly to a pitch and then clipped suddenly to emphasise the vastness of eternity.' Nader saw all this and believed it. He gave me back my hand, adding confidently, 'There is no hell, Koko; hell is here, now. Hell is war. Famine. Disease. Lust. Treason. They're all here for us to endure, my friend.' To my amazement, his voice was now coming from a clear source I'd never heard before. It had no more scratches, no air bubbles. This must have been his original voice, the one that oiled the chords of his throat before the asthma and drugs shredded it. I listened, rapt, as he continued, moving into an elaborate metaphor, imagining Life as a train gliding out of Central Womb, traversing the pastureland of Childhood in a carriage of long sleeps and bright dreams (he was half-humming that bit). Then, approaching Puberty, swerving a little, shaking a little, letting in the dreams, letting them sneak into your body, your flesh becoming your best friend and worst enemy. (He clenched his fists close to his chest hugging an imaginary sweetheart.) After that, Mount Maturity – mind the gap – change stations, look for new connections, start catching insidious germs from seedy passengers: ambitions, opportunities, goals, achievements, careers, successes. Your determination some-times ruthless, oblivious to the passing of time, believing that you own millions of tomorrows. (He chuckled dryly.) Soon, often too soon, Junction Fifty, and bumps, sudden descents beginning to mar the ride. Ho, ho, hold on to your seat, don't rush back looking for earlier carriages, grab at the windowsills and learn how to whisper lies into your nightly pillow. And oh, much sooner than you dreamt of, desolate grey hamlets will begin to roll by, on and on, with scratched-out names and scant passengers dragging their feet and their meek luggage. You forget whole chunks of your life as if you'd seen them on the stage in a foreign language. You'll collide with a former lover and un-wittingly curse the clumsy stranger. You'll look at photos of yourself on your mother's lap and squint hard but your clarity will have long gone. Then will come the moments of terrifying nose-dives when you wake up from a slumber staring at the ominous darkness of Terminal Finalis looming in the distance towards you.

He was swelling like a loaf of bread in the oven, and yet his temperature was still low. He pulled my hand again and kept it resolutely on his chest. The astonishingly thunderous beat of his heart reverberated through me as he rasped:

'Carry nothing; keep none of your petty stock
Thus thou break with ease your earthly lock
Meet your Shepherd on the highest rock
Watching forever His grazing flock.'

Was it one of his many memorisations, or was he actually improvising? Nader whispered the last few words and passed out.

14

A shadow spread over us.

I looked up . . . and straight into a hallucination. It was the witch on her white donkey, her white sherwal-camis rippling in the wind. A halo of red hair flamed around her face. She said something, the words inaudible but the feline timbre of her voice strangely familiar. She was staring at me as if into a mirror. I stared at her in return. My mind blacked out for a moment. Then, 'Najla? Is that you?'

'Hello, Koko.'

'What are you doing here?' I cried.

The past had suddenly become present and was even now dismounting and kneeling on the grass beside our shared nemesis.

'So he finally managed to smoke his life away,' she said, contemplating Nader's face.

I imagined Nader waking up and seeing this angel of death hovering over his sagging soul. What would he do?

Najla slipped her fingers under his neck searching for a pulse. I don't know if she found any. Then she closed her eyes and began breathing deeply. At first she clasped her hands as if in prayer. All her fingers had rings. Then she started to rub her hands together briskly. The more she rubbed the calmer her face became. Her eyelids were so still she appeared to be in a trance. I watched, bewildered. It must have been ten minutes before she stopped rubbing her hands. They were now as red as coals. She raised her head high, filling her whole body with air, and remained motionless for a few seconds. Then she dug her feverish palms into Nader's chest and pressed firmly, discharging the captive air. Nader's body was hit with a charge that made him judder. He emitted a long gurgle and began to cough.

'Help me, Koko,' Najla gasped, gesturing at Nader's head. I slid my hand under his neck and knelt behind him. Then I lifted his shoulders and let his back lean against my stomach. He felt slightly warmer than before. Najla continued breathing rhythmically, perhaps to regain the energy she had just lost. But was this Najla for real? Her size was imposing – she was double the woman we had both loved. So well I had known her, so little connection between us now. It made me doubt my own memory.

Najla's donkey snorted close to Nader's face. Najla opened her eyes and waved her hand at its muzzle. The donkey shook its floppy ears and showed its teeth before backing away.

'How Biblical, hey?' I joked, in a feeble attempt at breaking the strange spell she was creating. 'All we need now are a few palm fronds and a bunch of urchins.'

Najla was as unresponsive as Nader. She closed her eyes again, reverting to her inner business.

A spasm of anger towards both of them silenced me. I shot a savage thought to Nader: I don't know what your darling Najla is doing to you, Maestro, but my gut feeling is that she's evoking a cosmic ban on any future encounter with you, here or in the hereafter.

'Be quiet, Koko, please.'

I looked up, startled. Had I been speaking aloud? Najla's face was awash with tears. She was trembling.

'Did you love him?' I demanded.

'I loved you more. But you are a mean Armenian bastard.'

'I should kill both of you.'

'You wouldn't kill a fly.'

'How would you know?'

'I know what I see. Here he is, at your mercy. Why don't you snap his neck?'

She was right. My mental crimes remain uncommitted. And now, hearing her voice and looking closely at her face, I had no more doubt that she was really here.

The three of us, together again.

The roar of an engine startled us both. A utility truck was juddering across the green plateau. I could see Am Hussein driving, Abla in the passenger seat.

I eased Nader forward and gestured Najla to hold him while I stood up. She cupped her palm behind his head like a baby's. My own hand could still feel the vulnerability of his neck – that neck I was supposed to snap to prove I had it in me to kill – as soft as dough, as fragile as an eyeball. Najla held Nader in her arms with a disarming tenderness. Her red curls covered her lowered face. La Pieta, but with Judas and Mary Magdalene.

Behind the truck, Hikmat was cantering the black stallion. He overtook his dad and slid off the horse near me. His brow was dotted with sweat.

'Wajeeh and Ahmad send their greetings.' He dug his hand in his pocket as he spoke, then produced two copper bullets. 'Souvenir. One for you, one for Hamlet.'

'What for?'

'To remember today. They said: There is a bullet waiting for all of us. Better to have it in your hand than in your heart.'

'Where are they?'

'Escorting the newlyweds. Give me your keys. I'm sorting out your cars.'

I handed him the keys to my car. He took them and jumped on his horse, grabbing the donkey's reins and dragging it along in a slow trot. 'Yalla, off to the doctor with you!'

With the sun gone down, the wind had become bitingly cold. Am Hussein stopped the truck and stepped out. 'Will he live?' he asked calmly.

Najla nodded.

Together we carried the martyr from the battlefield and laid him on the pile of tents in the back of the truck. As ever, between Najla and me.

The truck lurched through the steep foothills. Nader's mouth was frozen in a silent scream. He didn't stir, didn't move a muscle. From time to time he startled us with a sudden snort, but having to clutch the sides of the truck prevented us from tending him as closely as his condition warranted.

We were headed towards the main road to Zahleh. The nearer we came to the valley, the more the wind eased, condensing the potent aromas of the plantations. The far-off mountains pulled closer together than during the day, tightening their grip over us. When the truck hit the level roads we drew closer to Nader again. Najla felt his forehead. She nodded very slowly. There was still some temperature in his skin, she said, but not much. 'Lukewarm, like fresh yogurt.'

Was he leaving us, cradled in this pile of tents, a baby Moses gliding away on the soft ripples of the Nile, going where there's no need for drugs, no hangovers, no side effects, no hankering for more?

Well, I have news for you Maestro. You can't die today. Today is not your day. The 13th of April belongs to other people. Whatever memorials are held on it in future, they will never, not in a hundred years, be yours. You ought to be appreciated, given the eulogy you deserve. So April 13th is a bad, bad choice. Who's going to give a shit about an artist whose life was dwarfed by civil war and who never reached his potential and who died on the second anniversary of a national disgrace? Choose a brighter day, Maestro, choose a humdrum day when your star can shine. Imagine newsreaders biting their elbows to find an exciting item, a breather to perk up their dull bulletin. Your passing would be bliss for them. What do you say to that? Anyway, it's too soon. Didn't you once say that if Shakespeare came to Lebanon he'd see 'the whole world is a stage' on display for real? Blood and treason and treachery and deception and heartbreak and lies and fratricide – the lot. Just hang in there. Imagine you and the Bard watching all his dramas mixed together on 10,450 square kilometres of the most illustrious set ever created. Wouldn't you rise from the dead for this? Come on, what are you doing, man? Pull yourself together. Don't quit so soon. The show has just begun. Besides, you have to see Nishan. He's walking today. First he just sat, sat and watched his chubby legs. Then he started holding on to the furniture and practising. And then he thrust himself into the void and waddled, balancing with his arms, pushing his neck forward. It's quite something, to rise up from the ground, step onto it, and use it to move on. Like a second birth. Come on Maestro, let's stop the bullshit, OK? I'll be frank with you: you demolished your own life. I'm sure you loved life, but you loathed the times we're going through so much you ended up a brawling foul-mouthed Messiah. Your pain turned you against yourself, against others too. You hurt the softest and closest targets to you. But this is you. So come on now. There's still work to be done. Get your shit together for God's sake.

I offered my hand to Najla over his body. She took it and topped it with her other hand, but I was reaching out like someone thirsty drinking in a dream. I wanted her to team up with me from the heart. I needed to feel her living soul again. I closed my eyes and willed her a message: Come, show me your spirit. But her palms between mine remained unresponsive, calm, and far, far away.

Her silence was becoming a lead casket. Long unbearable moments passed. I wanted my hand back but was nervous of retracting it with no reason. I noticed a joint protruding from Nader's denim jacket. I retrieved my hand at a snail's pace and took the joint.

The first draw invaded me in a thick blur. Then a tepid

shower drenched my insides. The second puff hammered my temples so hard I could hear my veins hooting in my head. My throat clenched. 'What is this?' I could hardly articulate the words.

'Pass it to me,' Najla said, reaching across Nader.

Uncertainly, I sucked at the joint again and passed it to her. She held it between the tips of her fingers, closed her eyes and drew slowly until it was all gone. Then she flicked the butt away.

My neck disappeared. 'What's in the joint, Najla?'

'Pure resin, pure opium, coke paste.'

'Jesus!'

My vision pulsed and dissolved before me, within me, I couldn't tell. The spaces between seemed immeasurable. The night awoke from its hibernation. The air was pierced with shivers of light rippling all the way to remote hamlets. Half-thoughts and reflections mingled in my distorting senses. I could feel the day's load dissipating, the whole day washing away. Gone was the hard separation from Nishan, the tension inside the elevator, the anguish of Manal's death and the gruesome reunion with Nader. All gone, as if a curtain had been drawn and then opened on a vast and endless space. I wasn't there any more. I was an imitation of myself. An envoy from Koko to Wonderland. The notion, coupled with the intense glowing of the trees fleeting past, enthralled me and lifted me so high that Nader was reduced to a match box, a purple aura outlining his hazy miniature body. My scalp was a hat about to fly. My pores dissolved into tiny bubbles of ecstasy. I was vaguely aware that my senses were tricking me, but the effect was so euphoric, it gave me wings.

I looked up at Najla. She was contemplating me, nodding, perhaps at last believing I was there. I smiled. She kept nodding, as if listening to a song in her head. I saw her dancing the Tamzara at Tony's. I saw her stepping naked into a lake, a silver waterfall glittering behind her. My eyes clung to her face. The more I stared the closer she was coming into our unforgettable beginning, into the spark of that magic encounter, when love was the great dissolver of boundaries and circumstances, when we copulated like creatures freshly forged by nature, triggered by a word, a song, a glance, a glass of wine, a failed painting, a triumphant success – making love becoming the subject and object of our very existence, crowning our days and our nights, afternoons and mornings, in sickness and in health, till Nader did us part.

I would have stepped over his prone form but I was liquid – liquid and steel. The changes in my body chemistry were ushering in the best Koko I'd ever known. I was transcending my reluctance to act from the gut. Everything was now possible, available, within arm's reach. The cautious and considerate Koko was being overwhelmed by the Armenian renegade. I was falling back into an era of myself that I thought had been eradicated. And I was rising up to the challenge. The sweet drive of yearning overpowered the years, and on a starless night on an empty road, in a country that has known peace only in its dreams, I was reclaiming my Najla. Her lips regained their original sensuality, her eyelids half closed over a spark of request. I have no memory of how I crossed to her, but she took me in her arms like a river takes a fallen leaf. She held my head with both hands, pushed me away, staring fiercely in my face, then pulled me back, clasping me tightly, tenderly. The thrust was harsh, burning. It brought a flow of colour into Najla's face, lighting it up with the wonder of love.

We floated through the darkness in a receding shimmer of dope and desire. Not a glimmer of light, not a flicker, not even a firefly in the scrubland along the road. The few willows among the cypress trees, their silvery leaves trembling, only amplified the immensity of the night. We were two pieces of ember ashing together. I had no idea how long we had coupled or whether we'd had fulfilling sex. My body wasn't answering questions or my mind ready to inquire.

Najla burrowed her head in her arms and turned her back to me. My throat was so dry I could have rung a bell with my tongue, yet I managed to mutter, 'Najla, what happened?'

'Nothing, Koko.'

Pause.

'I mean, after you disappeared?'

She stirred only slightly and took a long time before answering. 'I survived as best I could.'

Her broken voice silenced me. I could feel her leaving me again, drifting towards Nader. She shuffled away and sat beside him. She held his wrist, her thumb feeling for his pulse with mounting desperation. He looked lifeless. Only the whites of his eyes showed beneath his half-shuttered lids. I felt a stab of panic and moved back to him.

'He's cold, Koko. I can't find his pulse. He's freezing.'

I touched his hand. He was indeed cold. The air jammed in my lungs. His cheeks were dry, his lips bloodless. The smell of the honey and eucalyptus gel he rubbed on his asthmatic chest had gone, leaving the stench of stale sweat.

'What?' Najla demanded.

'What what? He may be dead – I don't know.'

'No!' She shook him frantically.

Her panic got to me. His utter helplessness got to me. I yanked at the edge of a tent and brought it over to cover the three of us, cutting off the cold wind. We pushed against him from both sides to give him some warmth. My inner pleading with him flooded my face with hot tears. I wasn't thinking, just listening to my heart.

I was sweating under the heavy canvas. A dull throb consumed my skull, thumping my ear drums. Somehow I knew that he

149

was still there. Perhaps there's a subconscious communication between people who love or hate each other.

There was a knock on the little rear window of the truck. A knock from the world we had forgotten. We looked at each other like criminals who'd been waiting outside a court room and now our case was being called. Abla's face was pressed to the glass. She was saying something but her voice was lost beneath the roar of the engine. Then she gestured: meet me halfway. I crawled to the edge while she craned her head out of the window, letting the wind unscarf her golden hair.

'How is he doing?'

'Not too good.'

'We're nearly there.'

'I think he's . . .'

'We're almost there.'

15

Zahleh was rattling with the ominous, invasive sound of generators. The Bride of the Bekaa was looking more like a derelict tramp dissected by a stinking rivulet that had once roared silver and inspired poetry. Only a few shops were still open, dimly lit. The truck continued westward along the fringes of the city, passing a series of closed shops and burned cars and suicidal cats oblivious to oncoming wheels. Then the elegant stone building of Zahleh's public hospital loomed up, ablaze with light.

As the truck engine stopped, Nader released a faint sigh. That small glimmer of hope knocked me onto my feet although my whole body was numb. I jumped recklessly from the back of the truck, hitting the ground almost on all fours. A male nurse and a nun rushed out with a wheeled stretcher, lifted Nader down and hurried him inside. Najla stumbled along behind them. She reached out to lift Nader's dangling right arm to his side, but the nun did it before her. I followed, treading hard on the cement floor.

'One person only,' snapped the nun. She pushed Najla before her through a flapping door, giving me a cold, halting stare.

I lingered in the foyer, rejected and edgy from the receding effect of the joint. Hospitals are anathema to me. I hate them even when they save my life, even in happy times. When I was shot in the shoulder I kept screaming at Emile to take me home; I dreaded overworked medics handling me roughly in their haste. When Arsiné was in labour, no one in her family or mine could persuade me to sit down. Fathers were not permitted in the delivery room. There was a wall between me and Arsiné. I fidgeted against that wall so much that by the end of the night my blue jacket had become white. Finally I barged in to see this little hairy creature all wrapped in a towel, suckling at my wife's breast. She lifted her gaze, smiling, pale but triumphant like a long-distance swimmer at the finish line. Yet all I could think of was getting her and the baby out of hospital and back home.

And now – it suddenly dawned on me – she would be pale with worry. I hurried to Reception. A young woman was just starting her shift at the front desk, buttoning up her white apron. The badge on her chest read Eva. She gave me a wait-a-minute look.

'All I need is a phone call, please.'

'Where to?'

'Beirut.'

'Are you with the new patient?' She gestured towards the resuscitation ward.

'Yeah.'

'Fill in this form for me.'

'I will fill in ten forms if you give me the telephone.'

'You can try, but the lines are playing up. "Repairs", they say.' She gave me the phone, buttoned the last button, took a book and an apple from her handbag, crossed her legs and began munching her apple as she read. The noise grated. Even worse was an alarm clock near her bag, ticking loudly. My uncle's ancient clock used to give me insomnia. I'd climb on my sofa-bed to stop its pendulum.

I lifted the receiver. The bulky black Ericsson added its 'normal' static to the annoying duet of apple and clock. I waited. A couple of minutes went by with no change, no sign of tonality. Sometimes an engaged bleep would emerge if the lines were under pressure; try several times and more often than not you get through. Not this time. Finally I gave up on my home number. I tried my uncle's. Same shit. I tried a special staff-only line the newspaper kept confidential for crucial calls.

The static was so loud I couldn't keep the receiver at my ear. I tried again. And again. I feared losing my temper or swearing. I took a biro from the counter and began filling in the form.

Name: Nader Abi Nader.
Address: Clemenceau, West Beirut.
Medical history: Asthma.
Occupation: Artist.
Contact in case of death –

I had no idea what to put down. Finally I scribbled Fathy's name and the *Daily Sun*'s phone number.

I pushed the form back to Eva: 'Can I have a slice of your apple? I'm starving.' I just wanted her to stop crunching it for a second. The crunching and the ticking were stretching my nerves wire-thin.

She looked at me quizzically, then offered me a whole apple from her bag. I joined in the noise to muffle the ticking.

'What are you reading?'

She flipped the cover: Lebanon in History.

'What does it say?'

'The whole book?'

'Just give me the gist.'

'It's saying that Lebanon is more like a state of mind than a real nation.'

'Thanks for the apple.'

'Are you Armenian?'

'I'm Koko, heard of me?'

'You took that picture of – '

' – the Israeli ass.'

The whole country still remembers a click that could have cost me my job, but hardly anyone ever mentions my other pictures. An Israeli ass has more impact on the collective Lebanese memory than the terrified faces and shredded flesh of its own people. Fuck the Pasha.

Najla came down the hospital corridor, red-eyed. 'He's in a coma, Koko, but the doctor says there's a chance he can hear us.'

'There's a chance? What exactly does that mean? If he can still hear, is he able to regain other faculties? Or is he going to fade away, hearing everything but unable to say a word? What kind of torture would that be?'

'Don't shout.'

I binned the apple core and hurried to the ward with Najla. Fuck the nun.

There were tubes all over Nader. A large dented hose coming out of his mouth distorted his bluish face. A grey-haired doctor was poking Nader's feet with a needle. The left leg twitched. The doctor's face registered the reaction. He wrote something on his clipboard.

'Is he going to make it?'

My voice irritated the medic. He looked at me, hard. 'And who might you be?'

'The one who signed the papers.'

'This is Koko, his only friend, Doc,' she said, her voice an olive branch. She laid her arm on my shoulder.

The doctor relented a little. 'We're doing our best.' He adjusted his stethoscope and began tapping Nader's chest. He took his time. When he stopped, he crossed his arms and kept looking at Nader, his eyes narrowing as if Nader was sailing away and he was straining to log his position. Then he turned to me: 'Stay with him for a while. Talk to him. Try to hit a sensitive cord. The shock is still fresh. He might respond.'

Nader's beetle-browed eyes were floating in a still orbit. 'Look at you,' I fumed under my breath. 'The Maestro! You inflicted this on yourself. You must have known you would implode sooner or later, yet you just kept rolling downhill.' The tube in his mouth twitched a fraction. 'Now you want to talk? What do you want to say? "Screw me for I have been a big shit?" Just look at you.'

The doctor turned to leave, murmuring something to Najla. She walked to the doorway with him.

Aunty Clauda used to warn me when, in a moment of rage, I cursed someone to hell: 'Don't say those things out loud, Koko, fate has big ears.' I never believed her, but now I felt Nader's fate was heeding my angry words.

The bullets poked at my thigh. I took them out and held them before his eyes: 'The outlaws sent their regards. One for you, one for me. If you don't pull through, I'll bury yours with you. There . . . ' I inserted one bullet into his fist and put the other on the bedside table for him to see. 'Keep looking at it and you'll pull through.'

My legs buckled beneath me. I dropped heavily onto a stool near the bed. My head felt so heavy I couldn't hold it up. I let it sink on to the pillow next to Nader. Half my mind restarted dialling Beirut. The static came back, along with the ticking of the receptionist's clock, her munching, the engine drone of the truck, the gunshots from the wedding, Yousef's flute, the filtered voice of Abla. Then Arsiné's face filled my vision, her gaze firmly focused with those black, black eyes, as if expecting the sun to rise. Nishan's little face surged from her gaze and I flew to him. I was leaving my body, drifting away. The weak light coming from the corridor seemed to grow brighter, filling my vision and growing stronger and stronger until it erased the room and all its boundaries. From a blurry point near where the floor should be, I saw my boss' shoes, his shiny black shoes. Then his grey trousers, pressed to a sabre's edge. He walked to me and stood his silent ground. And still I couldn't say a word, as if we were still in this morning's elevator. In his right hand he held Nader's notebook. A congratulatory smile trickled on to his sad face. He nodded, put the notebook in his pocket and bent over to take the camera from my lap. I let go of it, though it felt as if he was pulling it from the cage of my chest. Then he turned and walked away, floated away, in his little white ballet shoes.

Epilogue

Nishan was four years old when Arsiné took him to London in December 1980, seeking sanctuary on humanitarian grounds. At Heathrow, two officers escorted them into a confinement room. 'It might take some time,' one of them said.

The sudden vacuum around her during those long hours of waiting felt worse than Beirut's chaos. But she needed stability, not chaos, stability in a system that would pave the way for Nishan's future. She had to accept that compassion was not going to be personalised but regulated by law. No one would rush to comfort her tearful boy and no stranger would ever take a moment to think of the world she'd lost. Had I gone to Armenia, she reflected without regret, I would have landed on friendly soil. People would have been there for me, understanding what I've been through and where I've come from. But what is there in Armenia for my son?

She'd lost Koko on one of the worst days of fighting in Beirut's Centre Ville. He was shot in the back from a little window of the Grand Theatre, a domed building in the Italianate style that had become a nest for snipers. The maw of a tank's gun was his last click.

Arsiné wanted a family-only funeral, but Uncle Varouj wouldn't hear of it. Hundreds flooded the Armenian Bishopric in Antelias, filling the large cathedral and the surrounding courtyard. They stood in line to pay their condolences one by one. They took Arsiné in their arms. They kissed her cheeks. They moaned and sobbed before her. She had no idea who most of them were.

The *Daily Sun* mourned its son, spreading his prize-winning shots over two pages with an obituary by Burhan Sadik:

Krikor Krikorian was a photojournalist. But first and foremost he was an artist with passion and conscience. His creativity earned him a position at the *Daily Sun* when he was only seventeen. It also earned him distinguished prizes. His portraits were compared to the work of Yousuf Karsh, while his precision and finesse with light reminded us of Manoug, two great Armenians like him. Koko was also a hunter. More often than not he made his decisions in the heat of the moment. His own ideas were his best achievements. His days and his hours belonged to his lens. During the first Israeli incursion he was trapped behind enemy lines for three days. We believed he had been captured or killed. When he showed up, bruised and in a damaged car, he walked straight to the dark room. That day Krikor brought home the closest takes of armoured vehicles and Israeli personnel ever caught by an Arab camera. But danger was not his only forte. His love of nature soon became apparent throughout the Arab press. Other newspapers began publishing shots unrelated to current affairs, just for beauty and pleasure. He chased butterflies and migrant birds as well as stray cats and lost children. He followed the flame everywhere, the flame of compassion and the flame of darkness. This click man was above all a true fire stealer. He belonged to the best minds of his generation: those artists and writers unjustly circumscribed by a vicious war.'

Sayfeh was fast becoming a ghost neighbourhood left to militias and contraband thugs, an Ali Baba cave for drugs, counterfeit currency, false documents, kidnapping and ransom negotiations, even a dubious blood bank. The local militia ruled the streets. They broke into houses whose occupants had fled and they looted everything, selling carpets and silverware and paintings to dealers. Their law? 'Those who escaped get what they deserve.'

Sporadic shelling spread to every corner of Beirut. Arsiné's home had been brushed by mortars several times. She sold the apartment for next to nothing. Her friends and Koko's were dispersing into the clouds of war. Emile left the *Daily Sun* to work in the Gulf. Staying with her parents or with Varouj and Clauda was only a short term solution; they were preparing their return to Armenia. The old country they'd once fled as children in search of safe haven was now opening its arms to them in their old age. But Arsiné had no nostalgia for a home-land she'd never known.

When she finally talked to the immigration officer, she felt as if Koko was inhabiting her voice, speaking in photographs of caved-in buildings, grey walls pocked with bullets, gouged by mortars, sprayed with blood. She said that her grandparents had escaped the Ottoman army when her parents were barely older than Nishan today, that they had carried their terrifying memories throughout their lives and she was hoping to spare her son similar scars. She emphasised that she wanted a job, not handouts. 'Any job is fine,' she said.

As a single mother, she was given a decent one-bedroom flat and a healthcare card. She had just enough English to get by. She cleaned in a pub and washed dishes in a restaurant until she was offered a steady position in a nursing home. In no time her rapport with the geriatric patients won their confidence. She eased her own grief by giving them time and attention. She found it soothing to hear stories about normal lives. Men who'd done the same job for sixty years, stayed married to the same woman, lived in the same house, had children whose future was clearly mapped out. And women who'd been through the Second World War, taken care of the wounded and helped rebuild their cities and their factories. Normal lives free of dislocation and destitution and uncertainty. She told them stories about Lebanon and Armenia and Koko, entrusting them with messages in case they met him clicking away on The Other Side.

No matter how much she craved a companion, Nishan came first. Year after year she wrote to charities asking for supplements to finance the expensive education she wanted for him. She'd recount the story of her husband killed during the civil war, citing incidents of his bravery, enclosing copies of his most memorable clicks. 'He paid with his life in the line of duty,' she'd write.

Their flat in Battersea was full of Koko's prize-winning photos. His trophies glowed in a glass-fronted cabinet together with the Presidential medallion that was laid on his casket. The cameras he used were also displayed. But the day Nishan announced his intention to take a course in photography at school and join a club for amateurs, Arsiné became agitated. She wanted him to be proud of his father, yes, but she didn't want him to take after him.

'Mum, stop worrying,' Nishan said. 'You gave me an opportunity Dad never had. I'm going to make you the proudest mother in the world.'

'Promise?'

'Yes! Now go – go check out that Chelsea flower show, it's the last day.'

Arsiné didn't like to leave him alone in the flat, but he didn't share her love of cultural events of any kind. He favoured activity and open spaces where he could ride his bike and kick a football around with his friends. Right now there was a football game coming up on TV and her fidgeting was getting on his nerves.

'It's raining,' she objected, scanning from the window the soggy green of Battersea Park.

'You going to let a little rain stop you?' he teased.

Reluctantly, Arsiné put on her raincoat and walked down Albert Bridge. The white railings of the bridge seemed to compensate for the grey sky and the muddy water beneath. One day I will be part of this city, she confided to the river. Her English was improving by the day. She rarely spoke Arabic or Armenian except with Nishan. English, the whole world was speaking English, and she was beginning to detect the different shades of slang, hidden meanings, insinuations and humour, drinking in a whole new culture in big thirsty gulps. What's more, she was enjoying it. She even enjoyed her job. Arranging flowers in the hall as well as decorating every room to the taste of its occupant at least gave some scope for her creativity, though she craved more. Her dream was to open an oriental boutique in Chelsea, but that would have to wait until Nishan was at university.

A bus covered in flowers drove by. A half-naked young woman painted in wild colours waved from its deck. Arsiné waved back almost like a native. It made her feel good to belong, albeit for a fleeting moment. At the beginning, she'd had problems with some of the less attractive manifestations of English eccentricity: the streaker running across a football field, the multi-coloured dreadlocks and body-piercings, the rag queen smelling of an abandoned slaughterhouse in the tube. She couldn't understand them, let alone explain them to Nishan. But she'd learned to accept them and even to enjoy the variety of this foggy, out-rageous city.

The sun came out as she was approaching the exhibition entrance and lifted her heart, but the long queue at the gate dimmed her anticipation. Crowds of people waiting and waiting reawakened memories of all those terrifying queues at Beirut bakeries when she feared blood and bread might mingle at any moment. She abhorred queues and began dreading the wait. What's more, the queue was moving at a snail's pace. The Lebanese tradition of elbowing your way to the front nagged at her like an unreachable itch. But the thought of a whole nation indulging in beauty just for the sake of it motivated her to be patient. She stood there imagining thousands of landscape artists, horticulturalists and garden designers dedicating months to creating an ephemeral paradise. She remembered from last year the abundance of colour that seemed to transform everyone, how even the greyest of people gained an exotic aura from their surroundings. And the scents, the childish joy of burying her nose in all those glorious flowers.

A Niagara of fragrance was cascading in her memory when a clap of thunder startled her and the rain began to fall in earnest. Arsiné covered her head with her raincoat hood and walked on towards King's Road sheltered by the shop awnings.

A nearby gallery was exhibiting the paintings of Najla Helou. Arsiné had deliberately missed the opening and the first week, when the painter would be hovering, soaking up the praise. Personal sensitivity aside, she wanted to be alone with those paintings, to have time to study them in peace. The critics had described 'a love triangle in a circle of fire made of violence, drugs, and despair.' And, 'Miss Helou is a living example of survival and hope from a generation of Lebanese artists largely marginalised by the civil war.' Arsiné had read all this and had followed closely the works of the Lebanese pioneers in painting and sculpture. Najla Helou belonged to the second generation, a generation that was crushed by the civil war before reaching its potential, scattered all over the globe and largely forgotten, overshadowed by younger, more commercially-motivated new-comers. Nevertheless, Najla seemed to have hung on with remarkable tenacity.

Arsiné had mixed feelings about Najla. She regarded the men who fell for her as victims of a ruthless seductress, but she couldn't deny Najla's appeal in a society where sexual freedom was akin to prostitution. Men had flocked to her apartment like wasps to honey, whether she indulged them or not. But none of her lovers had lasted more than a couple of months. Except Koko. That alone was enough to stir Arsiné's curiosity.

The exhibition was titled 'Breastless Virgins'. The play on words – Breathless/Breastless – brought a smile to her face. Whether it reflected the contents was another matter. Arsiné studied the picture in the window: a slender girl hovering in mid-air as if caught inside a whirling storm. Her body was bent from the middle, her arms curved above her head. Her expression was neither happy nor sad. An eternal question mark.

Inside, the gallery was, as Arsiné had hoped, nearly deserted, apart from an attendant reading a book at her desk and a couple of young tourists contemplating the many variations on the same theme. In each picture the girl's position was different. She was naked, waifish, unable to spread her arms fully, whipped by rough strokes of red, black and rusty grey. Flying and yet earthbound, as if longing to escape her wind-swept cage. Captivity and freedom were fused together in a cry for release. There was no hint of the war, nor any other figures to suggest a 'triangle'. Just one frail, vulnerable female trapped inside a passionately coloured chaos. What was she trying to convey?

The door opened and Najla strode in, smoking a thin cigarillo and wearing a shiny black raincoat and huge silver earrings, her hair bound in a red bandana. Her impossibly high heels beat a tattoo across the floor. Behold, the artist, Arsiné thought wryly. She carried on looking at the paintings, hoping to remain unnoticed. She liked being around painters, though she never wanted to become too close. There was something disturbing about them, as if their sensitive nature allowed them to unsettle everyone. She preferred the company of more down-to-earth crafts people like herself.

The young couple turned around and introduced themselves to Najla, enthusing about her work. They were interested in purchasing a piece: which one would Miss Helou recommend for a large living room with magnolia walls?

'The one you were just looking at,' Najla said, pointing over their shoulders. Then: 'Holy shit!' she exclaimed, rushing past them towards Arsiné. 'Are you who I think you are? Are you? You are! You haven't changed a bit, even the same hairdo!' she cried, engulfing Arsiné in her embrace. Arsiné stiffened for a moment, then found herself surrendering and holding Najla against her with equal fervour. In that instant she felt a magnetic force wiping away their estrangement, their common loss becoming a bridge between them.

'You know what? Koko was there when I started this collection,' Najla said through her tears when finally they released each other.

'There? Where?'

'In the wilderness of Lebanon.' She clamped Arsiné's hand in hers. 'I can't believe this is happening, slap me across the face,' she laughed. 'Hey, how's that son of yours?'

'Nishan is good, thanks.'

'Is he anything like his father?'

'Some things he does make me wonder.'

'Like what?'

'Like eating standing up in the kitchen unless I sit him down. Like jumping out of bed in the morning as if touched by a hot iron. The way he throws his coat on the chair the minute he steps into the flat. Little things like that.'

'Genes.'

How could a simple hairdo be such a hallmark of identity? Arsiné couldn't even recall when Najla had last seen her. At the Hamlet rehearsals? At the Horse Shoe? Koko's funeral? She'd never imagined, or particularly desired, meeting Najla, and yet now it felt inevitable, natural. They were scrutinising each other as if they'd just found something they'd lost a long time ago.

'How about a cup of coffee across the road?' asked Arsiné.

'I have a better idea. Come with me.' Not bothering to excuse herself from the bewildered buyers, Najla marched Arsiné outside and hailed a taxi.

Lightning was turning London's sky silver. The two women sat quietly together as the taxi made its way through the traffic. Arsiné marvelled at the workings of fate. If it hadn't rained, if she hadn't left the queue when she did . . .

Across Hyde Park and into Lancaster Gate, the cab snaked

through the leafy streets before letting them out in front of a multi-storey Edwardian building.

As they entered the foyer, Arsiné asked: 'You live here?'

'Yes. We moved to London two years ago.'

We? Arsiné wondered but refrained from asking.

At the end of a dusky corridor, Najla opened the door to her flat. It was glowing with subdued light from a small courtyard. The living room was crammed with clutter: vases in copper, earthenware, glass, and carved wood. Tiny ornamental mirrors, coffee cups, water pipes, piles of newspapers and art magazines. The walls were completely covered with paintings by her and other Lebanese painters like Guiragossian, Abboud, Khalifeh and Farroukh. Photos, artefacts, jewellery, postcards, Arabic miniatures. A Bedouin in London. Arsiné smiled to herself and sat on a sofa facing the French windows. The rain had stopped but the clouds were keeping the sun at bay.

Najla went to her table-bar and poured two glasses of red wine. She handed one to Arsiné and sat near her on the sofa. Najla stared blankly at the Oriental rug under her feet, cradling her wine. Arsiné guessed she was collecting her wits, so she kept her peace. After a long pause Najla blinked, heaving a long breath. She put her drink on the side table and claimed Arsiné's hand.

'I hated myself for making Koko fall in love with me. I so much wanted you to know that,' she said with emphasis. 'There was no chance I could make him happy. He knew that from the start. But he was an incurable romantic. He could give and give and ask so little in return. I was against monogamy. Still am.' She was breathing with difficulty. Arsiné remained calm, listening like a priest at a confessional. 'You see, Arsiné, to love someone as much as you love yourself, you need to share yourself with them. Koko expected that and deserved it. But I couldn't do it. I just didn't have it in me. Perhaps I needed every iota of myself to invest in my painting. And perhaps I was too preoccupied looking for the true me.' Najla picked up her glass. Her hand was a bit unsteady. 'I'm still looking. It's never going to end,' she added softly.

'Maybe you're too scared to find yourself? Maybe you nearly met yourself once or twice and turned away?'

'You're a shrewd woman.' Najla managed a wan smile. 'Hey, am I imposing on your schedule?'

Arsiné shook her head. Nishan's lunch was ready in the fridge. The football would keep him entertained until she got back. Suddenly she was glad she'd abandoned the flower show, and not just because of the rain.

Najla went to a desk and began shuffling through a pile of files and folders. Arsiné sipped her wine and watched. Here's the woman who propelled Koko into my arms after nearly destroying him. Should I love her or hate her?

Before she could make up her mind, Najla brought a large folder back to the sofa and laid it in Arsiné's lap. 'I'd like you to have the sketches from my time with Koko. Please.'

Arsiné said nothing. She looked through the sketches slowly, hoping to find the right answer. How she would explain them to Nishan was her first concern. And what would she do with them in the long run? They were better – less pretentious, more visceral – than the paintings they'd inspired.

While Arsiné studied the sketches, Najla talked about how she'd been pulled by two opposites: the mad and maddening Nader, the lively and gentle Koko. She loved them, each for himself and both for her own vanity. 'I had a breakdown soon after Koko stormed out. My work suffered a total block, so I put my belongings in storage and left for Yammouneh, in the hills overlooking the Bekaa Valley. My grandfather had left me a couple of stone cottages up there. No one had any idea of my whereabouts. Some believed I'd gone to France, others wondered whether I'd committed suicide or been kidnapped, or maybe I was hiding inside a Palestinian camp. In fact, all I was doing was wandering around that barren mountain. Some naïve villagers believed I was a witch. Yoga and meditation were sorcery to them. They'd see me lotusing on a rock completely tranced and deduce that I was connecting with Satan. But no one harmed me. As you know, there were only a few safe havens where you didn't feel the pressure of the war. Sooner or later someone you knew was bound to show up in one of them. So one day Koko and Nader showed up.'

'April 13th 1977,' Arsiné said, still turning pages.

'Yeah . . . ' The date brought a frown to Najla's forehead but she continued, 'Well, Nader had had too much to smoke that day. He was totally wasted. He passed out in the middle of the valley. When I found them, Koko was trying to revive him. We took him to hospital.' Najla lowered her gaze.

Arsiné had the feeling that Najla was editing her account, but there was no point pushing her for details. 'Koko told me he left Nader in a coma with you,' she said, setting the folder aside.

'He remained in a coma for fifty-nine days. I stayed with him. I couldn't leave him, you know. I stayed, talking to him, massaging his limbs, reading to him, spoon feeding him. Sometimes his eyes would speak volumes. It was so frustrating. I knew he was dying to talk. It distressed him that he might die without saying what he had to say. Then one night I heard his voice. I was sleeping on a narrow cot near him and thought I was dreaming. "Koko," he said – his voice was gurgling as if coming from the sea. "Close-up on the water." Two months in a coma and he was still shooting a film he never finished. But those were his last words.'

'He died?'

Najla stared at the rain gliding down the window. The thin lines of her eyelids were heavily painted in mauve, but it failed to camouflage the depth of those lines. Then she claimed Arsiné's wrist. 'Come with me,' she said.

Arsiné followed her down another dim corridor behind the

kitchen. The wooden floor creaked loudly. Electric cables and switches had been torn from their moorings, left awkwardly knotted or just hanging out from the walls. The creaking floor was uneven.

At the end of the corridor was a heavy wooden door. Najla pushed it open with her shoulder and beckoned Arsiné to enter.

Inside was a storeroom piled high with boxes and containers lining the walls. The only light came from a tiny red bulb and a shivering TV screen in the far corner. The smell of damp dust and medical disinfectant turned Arsiné's stomach. She took in a long breath just before the door closed behind her. Najla said nothing, just led Arsiné towards the centre of the room where a large leather recliner was facing the static TV. There was something in the chair. No, someone. Arsiné gasped. A minuscule grey-haired, bearded old man in a red robe was ogling the vacant TV with vacant eyes. In the dim light he could be mistaken for a pile of discarded clothes.

'Don't worry, Nader can't move. He can't talk, but he can see and hear,' Najla whispered. Then she knelt down near the man. 'We have a VIP for today's screening, Maestro,' she said. But his eyes remained still. Apart from a faint twitch in his fingers, he seemed frozen. A tiny object glinted in his clenched right hand.

Najla stepped towards the TV, took a deep breath and assumed an announcer's mien: 'Dear friend, it is my pleasure and my privilege to bring to you today a film about a history of survival; the survival of the Lebanese in their ancient and complex relation with the sea. It is not a long film. It is not entertainment. But it is a chunk of real life encapsulated in a few fabulously-edited shots. Watch and see. Observe and remember, because those who forget repeat their mistakes.' Najla was addressing Arsiné with all due seriousness, as if speaking to a crowded cinema. Then she bowed, pressed a button on the set and came to stand on the other side of the chair.

The dark screen stirred. At first Arsiné took the sound of waves for distant thunder, the surface of the sea for a sky before the storm. Then the shadows lifted into close-ups of swelling waves, showing ominous details of foam and rubble. The title rose from the deep in dripping red letters: Blue Pirate. An organ began a dissonant crescendo. The waves flickered as the scene began to expand, until hundreds of milky white horses broke into minute bubbles and the scene revealed a floating dead woman in a white dress cradled between dunes of water. Arsiné squatted, leaning closer to the screen. The camera rose slowly to rest on a distant horizon. A ferry boat appeared, moving closer as the music began another crescendo. The boat was laden with escapees. The camera juddered towards them, obviously struggling to stay focussed. A few people spoke from the deck. Furious. Disoriented. Saved but still lost. One man tossed his child in the air. The camera froze the toddler all alone against the vacant sky for several chilling seconds. The father held out his passport and stabbed the cedar tree on its cover with an angry finger.

This was followed by an abrupt cut to raw episodes of the uprooted and homeless, bereft of their children, orphaned, wounded, maddened by their sudden misery. A distraught mother dragged her three children through devastated alleys, leaving behind her a pancaked house. Their faces filled the screen to the point of distortion. The camera lunged at them aslant as they ran. They howled, engulfed by murky brown smoke. Another sudden cut: the thumping music diminished to a static hiss, bringing to the screen sharply-contrasted stills in black and white: a father hurtling out of a crumbling arcade, his child half-buried in the dust behind him; a little girl cradled by the rubble of her bedroom; a skinny mongrel sniffing at a bloated cadaver. The shots were held for twenty seconds each, carving their details onto the viewer's memory.

Then the sea again, as calm as a lake, with the camera plunging out of a burst of sunlight to fall back on the floating woman, her body now drumming the side of a boat, evoking desperate knocking on a deaf door. The music echoed the drumming and then faded away as the light slowly dimmed into a blank black screen.

A cold shiver ran up Arsiné's spine. Her knees felt weak and her mouth dry. She stood up, slightly dizzy, and looked at her watch: only ten minutes had passed. 'Powerful stuff,' she said. 'A relentless face-slapping.' She was uncertain what else to say and settled for 'Thank you for letting me see it.'

Najla moved to stand near her. She brushed Arsiné's shoulders with a soft gesture of gratitude. Then she leaned down and said to Nader: 'This is Arsiné, Maestro. Remember? Koko's wife?'

Slowly the dead eyes, webbed with red veins, stirred, then stilled again.

Najla put her hand in Nader's robe and extracted a copper bullet. His clenched fist began to throb. 'It's OK, Maestro,' she reassured him. 'We're giving her Koko's. No one is taking yours.' She handed the bullet to Arsiné. 'This is a talisman. Koko left it behind at the hospital.'

Arsiné received the bullet in the palm of her hand. It was warm, and heavier than it looked. 'Koko never mentioned a lucky-charm bullet. He must have forgotten it.'

'He didn't forget it. He placed it where Nader could see it. A challenge for him to stay alive.'

Arsiné slipped the bullet into her pocket. 'Thank you.'

Acknowledgements

Without the patient assistance of Lydia Smith this novel would still be in the limbo of my everlasting dissatisfaction. Elizabeth, my partner and companion, and my daughter Rouba are two more loyal soldiers who kept me in the field for five years. I'm grateful also to Hilary Simmons and Melanie Ensor for sending further munitions to the front. And deepest thanks to Naim Attallah for all his support.

The Author

Jad El Hage was born in Beirut and has been a journalist since he was sixteen, working for Al Hayat in London and Beirut, BBC World Radio in London, Radio Monte Carlo in Paris, and Harlequin Arab World (Senior Editor) in Athens. His work has largely focussed on the arts: reviewing books and covering numerous cinema and theatre festivals all over the world.

In 1985 he moved to Australia with his wife and two young daughters to join the rest of his family. He has been heavily involved in Australia's and Lebanon's arts scenes and has had one novel, six collections of poetry and two of short stories published in Arabic, as well as two plays staged. Parts of his work have been translated into French, German, Dutch and Spanish. He has also written two earlier novels in English: *The Last Migration* (2002) and *The Myrtle Tree* (2007).

He now lives in a small village in north Lebanon.